ACKNOWLEDGEMENTS.

I like to thank you Wayne Stapley, for the first edit, and your patience.

Thanks to my family and staff for your help and enthusiasm.

I also like to thank my friend Arie Brouwer, for sharing his childhood memories.

My brother in law Bart Smit and Jan Blauw, and the
Historische Vereniging, gemeente Diever, thank you.

Produced by·

FriesenPress
Suite 300 – 852 Fort Street
Victoria, BC, Canada V8W 1H8

www.friesenpress.com

Distributed to the trade by The Ingram Book Company

FOREWORD.

After enduring five years of brutal and deadly enemy occupation, the Canadians and their Allies marched into the Netherlands and brought the Dutch freedom.

On May 5, 1945, German General Blaskowitz signed the surrender of the German occupational forces of the Netherlands, in the city of Wageningen.

7,900 soldiers, 88,900 civilians and 106,000 Jewish compatriots had perished.

Every year at 8 p.m. on May 4, the Dutch commemorate civilians and soldiers, who have died in the Kingdom of the Netherlands and elsewhere in the world, with two minutes of silence.

On May 5, the day on which the people of the Netherlands were freed from the oppressive German yoke, liberation day is celebrated.

Thankfully, I didn't experience World War 2 personally, but have listened to the many stories told by my parents, the people around me when growing up, and the many veterans I met after residing in Canada.

I believe it's our job to pass on what happened during the war from generation to generation.

Those who don't know history are destined to repeat it.

Edmund Burke.

When greed sups with the devil
And principals are shed
When power is corrupted
And truth stands on its head
When fear pervades the confused mind
And fools are easy led
When reason is a prisoner
The bell tolls for the dead.
  Tom Walker.

For Jort and Niels.

ONE

2001.

Ann pushes the flashing button of the intercom.

"This is the second interruption Shana and it's only eight forty five! I've told you to hold all my calls! You know I have a deadline!"

"I'm sorry Ann, but you might want to take this; it's an overseas call and it seems to be important. I was told it's urgent."

Irritated, and somewhat alarmed, Ann picks up the receiver.

"Hello?"

"Annie? It's Josie."

"Josie? Is everything all right?"

"No, it isn't. It's Mamma—she had a major stroke and is in intensive care. Papa is with her, but I should get back to her room as soon as I can. I thought you might want to come home, if you can get away. I don't know if she'll make it Sis, it's very serious. Please come home as soon as possible. It…uh…maybe it sounds weird Ann, but it seems she's waiting for you…can you come?"

"Oh my dear God! Do I even have enough time? How bad is it, Josie?"

"It's not good Annie, I don't know if she'll pull through."

Her sister sounds tired and weary.

"It's a crazy time here right now, but I will come as quickly as I can. I'll get there with the next available flight. Hang in there Josie, okay? Please give my love to Papa. I'd better get off the phone now and get packed!"

"I carry my phone in my pocket; write the number down and phone me as soon as you get your ticket, okay? I'll arrange for somebody to pick you up at the airport."

Ann quickly jots down her sister's new cell phone number.

"I'll phone right away after my flight is booked, Josie."

She calls her secretary.

"Shana, I need an airline ticket to Amsterdam ASAP; connect me with Bob Stapley's office, please."

Her boss answers his phone. He sounds stressed and impatient.

"Yes, what is it, Ann?"

"I have to go to Holland, Bob."

"Holland? Why and when?"

"Today—I have to go today."

"Today? You must be joking! What the hell! Give me a break! We have to get that story out Barlow! No way in hell you can leave today!"

"I have to go, Bob. It's my mother. She had a stroke and is in serious condition. I'm almost done with the article. Henry can finish it and get it proofed in time."

"Shit, that's all I need today, but you have to do what you have to, I guess…and… uh…Ann, I'm sorry about your mother."

"I know, Bob."

"Now get out of here and have a safe flight."

Shana's intercom button lights up.

"I've booked a flight to Schiphol, Amsterdam, with the Dutch airline K.L.M., leaving Pearson at three fifteen this afternoon. You can pick up the ticket at the K.L.M. desk. May I ask what the emergency is Ann?"

"It's my mother, Shana. She's in the hospital in intensive care. I have to go home."

"I'm sorry to hear that, Ann. Is there anything I can do for you?"

"Yes please. Send Henry Jackson the story; he has to finish it. Assist him if he has any questions. I'll take my laptop; e-mail me if there's anything you need to know. I'd better phone my husband now. Thanks for your help, Shana."

She dials her husband's direct line, but is redirected to the receptionist.

"Barlow and Robson, how can I direct your call?"

"It's Ann Barlow. Please connect me with my husband's office—it's urgent."

"He is in meetings all morning, Mrs. Barlow, I…"

"Right now, please?"

"Carson here—what's so important, Ann? I'm in the middle of a conference."

"I'm sorry Carson, but I had a call from Josie earlier. It's Mamma; she had a stroke. I'm leaving from Pearson at three fifteen. Can you meet me there?"

"Oh dear, how bad is it?'

"It doesn't look good. Josie is worried she might not make it."

"I'll cancel all my meetings for today and I'll meet you at home. You do have to pack right? I will take you to the airport, okay sweetheart?"

"Thanks darling, I'll see you at home."

It's already after ten when she leaves the building's parkade. Of course the traffic is insane and she's a nervous wreck by the time she gets home.

Carson is at home packing her suitcase; he has put some cash and her passport on the nightstand.

"I don't know exactly what you want to take, but I got most of it, I think."

She throws her make-up and toiletries in a bag, and checks her suitcase to make sure that what she needs is packed.

"I've got your raincoat—you probably need it in Holland—and a pair of comfy shoes. Is there enough room? Here, let me help you," Carson says. He zips up the suitcase.

She quickly changes into a comfortable pair of pants, a loose top and a short blazer.

"We'd better go now, honey. Do you have your credit card and passport?"

"Yes, I'm ready—let's go."

She phones her sister on the way to the airport.

"There's no change, Annie; it still doesn't look good, but she's hanging in there. Bram Boonstra will pick you up at the airport. I'm so relieved you're coming."

"So am I Josie. I'm glad I was able to catch this flight. Try to relax, okay? There's nothing you can do now; try to get a bit of sleep—you sound tired."

"I'll try, Sis. See you when you get here. Love you."

"Love you too."

They make it to the airport just in time to check her suitcase.

"Thanks sweetheart. I wouldn't have gotten here this fast without your help. Please give the kids a hug. I'll phone as soon as I get to Amsterdam."

"Try to get some shut-eye if you can, honey. Keep me posted—and don't worry about things here at home, we'll be fine."

He walks her to the security check in. "I love you."

"I love you too," and she quickly walks through the gate.

She grabs a coffee and a muffin on the way to the waiting area, where she finds an empty seat near the window. She opens her computer and writes a short e-mail to Henry, her assistant, and explains where she's at with the article, and to ask Shana for help if he needs anything. Then she writes a quick note to her children.

I have to go to Holland; Oma is very ill. I will be back as soon as possible. Please be good for Dad and listen to Rosa. I will bring you some Dutch treats, the ones you like so much. Love you. Mom. xxoo.

She closes the computer, walks over to the window and watches the planes land and take off in a steady stream, taking their human cargo to destinations all over the world.

It's time to board the plane. She waits until most the passengers have passed the check-in desk before she hands her boarding pass to the friendly attendant. "Welcome aboard Mrs. Barlow. Enjoy your flight."

She locates her seat and is fortunate to have the whole section to herself. After putting her laptop and blazer into the overhead compartment, she takes a deep breath and sits down. *What a rat race! I would have never thought when I got up this morning that I would be on the plane to Holland this afternoon!*

The plane is ready for takeoff and taxis to the designated runway. It revs the engines, and as it picks up speed, pushes her back in her seat. Through the window she can see the airport and the city of Toronto get smaller and smaller. When the plane is in the air and stable, the flight attendant comes by and hands her the Herald. She flips through it but can't concentrate, and puts the newspaper in the pocket in front of her. The fluffy clouds she sees from her window calm her and she tries to relax. It's going to be a long nine-hour flight. After she enjoys a nice cup of tea, she asks the attendant for a blanket and a pillow. She wraps herself in the blanket, puts the pillow under her head, and closes her eyes.

TWO

In 1978, after studying for three years, Ann received her degree in English. Creative writing is her forte, and she wanted to pursue a career in journalism. When she's done her research, to find a school, she decided to go to the School of Journalism in Amsterdam.

She works part time as a waitress all the way through university. When she's finished her course, she has saved enough money for a trip to France with her two best friends, Sandy and Susan, before returning to school.

While camping in the south of France, she meets Carson Barlow, who is backpacking through Europe with a couple of his friends. It's easy to like the handsome, dark-haired Canadian young man. The girls spend almost two weeks with their new-found friends. They hike together, play beach volleyball, and visit the local clubs. Carson Barlow finds the blond-haired, green-eyed Dutch girl very attractive, and he and Ann try to spend as much time as they can away from the group.

While attending university in Toronto, Carson works part-time at the architect firm Barlow and Robson. He studies to be an architect—like his parents, Thomas Barlow and Catherine Robson.

He's funny and likes to tease her. She has no problem with that! She can give back as good as she gets, and the two of them make a good match. She's happy to have met somebody with so many similar interests. They love each other's company, and by the time the vacation comes to an end they're in love.

Her friends tease her about her summer romance, but Carson and Ann write each other every week. Carson has saved enough money to visit for her birthday, in May, and after spending some time together again, they realize their love for each other is real.

When Ann tells her parents about her plans to move to Canada a few months after Carson's visit, Mieneke and Peter Jansen are not happy with their daughter's decision. They do however like Carson Barlow and always kept a special place in their hearts for the Canadian heroes, who in 1945 liberated the Netherlands from the German occupation.

The wedding date is set for May 8, 1980.

Carson arrives in Amsterdam on April 28th, with only his parents, but it's agreed there will be a big celebration, with his siblings, friends and relatives, back home in Toronto.

Their parents get along great. Mieneke and Catherine both enjoy working on the wedding day preparations, and Peter and Thomas like each other's company. Tom takes a liking to the Dutch Heineken beer and the Dutch liquor Jenever. They talk often about the war. Wayne, Tom's brother, served in the Canadian Army and was in the city of Apeldoorn when Holland was liberated. The two men create a strong bond when visiting Apeldoorn together, and already talk about visits back and forth.

It's a beautiful sunny day when Ann and Carson get married. It's wonderful to see all her friends and relatives at the reception, and introduce them to Carson and his parents before they leave for Canada.

The entire family comes to Schiphol, Amsterdam's airport, to see them off. Ann is nervous and sad to leave her parents and sister, but she's also excited to start her new life. Her parents already have plans to come to Canada, and Josie says she'll save every penny she can to come for Ann's birthday.

"Please write to me often, Annie."

"I will, I promise."

They both cry when it's time for her to go.

THREE

It's tough to get started in her new country, and money is tight for the first couple of years.

They move into an apartment close to the university in Toronto, and Ann finds a job at a printing firm within walking distance from their home.

After her request to the school in Amsterdam to send her records to Toronto, she's accepted in the Toronto School of Journalism, ten months after her arrival in Canada. She applies at the Toronto Sun and gets a part-time job as an intern, and works hard to build her portfolio, first as a proofreader and then as an assistant to the editor. Juggling her time between school and the newspaper, Ann still finds time to write short stories, and sometimes they get published. The money is always more than welcome and is spent on cheap dinners out or on weekend camping trips.

When Carson is done university he starts working full-time at his parents' firm. Tom and Catherine are fair, but tough. They expect their son to work his way up the ladder like any other employee.

With her parent's financial assistance, Ann is able to go home for her sister's wedding and her grandparent's funerals.

She misses her family terribly, but Mieneke and Peter Dekker come for a few visits; Josie, who didn't manage to save enough money to come for her sister's first birthday in her new country, comes to Canada with her new husband in the summer of 1984, and they stay for an entire month.

Mieneke and Peter experience a real Canadian winter when waiting for the birth of their first grandchild.

Thomas Peter Barlow is born on December 11, 1986.

Shortly after their son's arrival, Ann is offered the position of staff writer at the Sun and she accepts, but only after Catherine insists to take care of Tommy.

When Carson is promoted to Principal Architect/Designer at Barlow and Robson, they decide to buy a house in the suburbs of Toronto.

On March 10, 1989, a blustery rainy day, the twins, Hanna Jennifer Barlow and and Catherine Wilhelmina Barlow complete the young family.

Ann takes a leave of absence after the birth of the twins, but after three months at home she's getting anxious to go back to work. They both agree that it's too much for Catherine to look after three children and, after some soul searching—torn between staying at home and going back to work—they decide to hire a nanny. They go through lots of interviews and follow up on loads of references, until it's agreed to trust Rosa Garcia with the children. It worries Ann every morning to leave her babies with a stranger, but after a few weeks she sees how the kids have warmed up to their nanny. When she notices how smoothly the Barlow family runs with Rosa at the helm, she's grateful, and feels sure that Carson and she made the right choice.

FOUR

A shrieking baby, three rows back, wakes her; she sits up when the flight attendant asks her if she can get her anything.

"We came by with dinner last night, but I didn't want to wake you. There are still some sandwiches, and there's coffee, tea or a glass of wine, if you like."

She does feel a bit hungry and asks the girl to bring her a ham and cheese sandwich and a coffee. She flips through the channels on the screen in front of her, but can't find anything interesting to watch. She feels anxious and is thinking of her mother. *Please don't go Mamma—not yet. We want to take you home,* she prays.

"Ladies and Gentlemen, we will shortly start our descent into Amsterdam. There's a light overcast and the temperature is eighteen degrees Celsius. Thank you for flying with K.L.M.; it was a pleasure serving you. Welcome home and, if you're a visitor, welcome to Amsterdam and enjoy your stay."

Through the wispy clouds she can see the concentric rings of the canals, and recognizes the Amstel River and the notorious Vondelpark in the distance, as the plane approaches the city of Amsterdam.

The sun, partially hidden behind the clouds, throws long shadows across the city, and although the harbor is enveloped in a slight haze, she can see the boats perfectly lined up. Small boats and big freighters come and go, and the streets below are abuzz with cars, buses and bicycles.

She's home.

Luckily, it doesn't take long to go through customs.

"Welcome to the Netherlands, Mrs. Barlow."

Bram Boonstra is in the arrival's waiting area. She hasn't seen him in years. He gives her a big hug.

"Welcome home Annie. I'm so sorry about your Ma; we all love her so much, and hope and pray that she'll pull through. You must be tired; let me get your suitcase, and we'll be on our way."

He has parked nearby in the covered parking lot and, with a skilled hand, he maneuvers his way out of the parkade; they're on the highway going north in less than fifteen minutes. It's a two-hour drive to get home. The traffic is crazy. Everybody drives at a high speed and people pass, dodging in and out the lanes, in quick jerky movements. She grabs her armrest and, white-knuckled, holds on tight.

Bram chuckles: "Nervous, Annie?"

"You guys are nuts here! Everybody drives like a maniac! It's like bumper cars!"

"Ah, you just forgot that you used to drive like this. You'll get used to it again."

"Holy, it scares the crap out of me! I'm glad I don't have to get used to this again, Bram," she laughs.

Traffic slows down when they get further north and leave the bigger cities behind, and the drive is relaxing her now. They are comfortable in each other's company and don't have to talk much. Farmland and meadows are spread out along the highway. It surprises her again how lush and green the grass is and how voluptuous the dairy cows are, with their udders and bellies almost touching the ground.

"How are your mother and your sister Liselotte, Bram?"

"They're fine. Liselotte moved back to Haarlem. She and her husband Jort work at the flower trading center there. My mother married Albert Hendriks after the war. You remember him? He used to be an Algebra teacher way back when."

"Yes, Mother told me they got married, and that she bought a house near you."

"Yes, Albert passed away a few years ago now, and mother bought a small house, kitty-corner from my wife and me, in one of the new divisions. She likes it and, of course, she never minded looking after the grandkids when they were little."

"Do you still hear from Klaus Berger, your friend from Germany?"

"Oh yes, Klaus and I stayed friends, ever since your great-grandfather found him behind the holly hedge!" Bram laughs. "We visit at least a couple of times a year. I'm surprised you still remember him!"

"When I was a little girl, I couldn't get enough of the story of how my mother and Opa found him after the war. I always cried because it was so sad. He was so young, too young to fight in a war! It's nice that you and he are still friends after all these years!"

They exit the highway and drive into the city.

"Do you want me to take your suitcase home or do you want to keep it with you, Annie?"

"I had better take it with me—you never know…"

"I'll come in with you; I want to see your Ma, if you don't mind. Maybe Uncle Peter needs something, but then I'll be on my way."

"Thank you so much for picking me up Bram, I sure appreciate it."

"No problem at all Annie, I'm glad I could help."

Her father tears up when he hugs her.

"I'm so glad you're here, Annie; how are you, and how are the kids?"

"Fine Papa—we're all fine, but worried. How are you and Josie holding up?"

"Papa is so tired, but he doesn't want to leave Ma alone," Josie whispers, when she hugs her sister. Ann takes her father's hand and they walk to the bed.

She hardly recognizes her mother. Her once beautiful thick blond hair is grey now and lies in a thin braid over one of her shoulders. Her cheeks are hollow and sunken. She's hooked up to all kinds of medical equipment and seems to be struggling for every breath.

"How is she, Papa?"

"I don't know if she'll make it, sweetheart. She had a major stroke. Now the doctor found fluids in her lungs too—that's why she's breathing so heavily. If she pulls through, her left side will most likely be paralyzed, and she might be in a wheelchair for the rest of her life."

Pa and Josie both look exhausted.

"The two of you should have some rest. Is there a visitor's room with a bed we can use?"

"Yes, there's a small room down the hall available. I told Papa to lie down for a while, but he doesn't want to."

"Please get me a coffee, Josie, and then you and Pa can have a bite to eat and go for a nap. I'll stay here first. We can take turns staying with Mamma."

Her father doesn't want to hear any of it.

"I'll stay here with her," he stubbornly says.

"Come on, Papa, we're only a few steps down the hall," Josie says.

Peter reluctantly gives in and leaves the room with his daughter.

Ann pulls up a chair and sits down beside her mother's bed.

"Mamma, are you awake? Can you hear me Ma? It's Annie, I'm here."

She strokes her mother's hand. There's no response. She takes her mother's hair-brush from the nightstand, takes out the braid and gently brushes the long, thin strands of hair. She keeps talking, telling her Ma funny stories about her children, and recalling memories from when she and Josie where growing up.

"Remember Ma when…"

Did she see her mother smile, or did she just imagine that?

Her mother stirs and tries to open her eyes. Her left eye stays closed, but Ann believes her mother can see her through her slightly-opened right eye.

"Annie, you came, that's good," she whispers with a slurred voice.

She reaches over and squeezes her daughter's hand, but then lays her head down again and closes her eyes.

The door opens just a crack and a nurse peeks in before entering the room.

"I hate to disturb you, but I have to change the sheets and give Mieneke a quick bath. Are you her daughter? You can stay, or you can get yourself another coffee," she says, when noticing Ann's empty cup.

"It's okay, I won't be in your way," Ann says. She gets up and moves to the end of the bed where she picks up her mother's chart—*Wilhelmina Dekker Jansen*.

"Go ahead, don't worry," the nurse says. "I'll be here till you get back. I'm going to be about fifteen minutes. The cafeteria is just around the corner. Take a break."

Ann gets a coffee from the machine and sits down at a table in the corner. *God, I'm tired*, she thinks.

"Peter Dekker, please return to room ninety-eight. Peter Dekker, room ninety-eight, please, right away," the voice over the intercom says.

Ann jumps up, spilling her coffee at the same time, but doesn't stop to clean it up. She meets up with Papa and Josie when she comes around the corner.

Nurses frantically work around the bed. Her mother gags when a nurse puts a tube in the back of her mouth to suck the fluid out of her throat. It's scary, and Ann feels so bad for her mother, and for her father, who must feel so hopeless to see his wife struggle for air.

After fifteen minutes, when the heart monitor and the oxygen supply are checked, and her mother's blood pressure has come down, a nurse gives her a needle.

They stand back, helplessly watching all the commotion.

Before the nurse leaves, she props her mother up with an extra pillow and checks the oxygen again.

"She seems to be calmer," she says; she straightens out the sheets, tidies up, and with a friendly smile adds, "The doctor will be with you shortly."

They sit close together around her mother's bed. The hours drag on. Her father doesn't want to leave the room. Josie and Ann take turns getting cups of coffee. Once in a while they doze off a little. Peter Jansen is the only one who never closes his eyes. He holds his wife's hand and strokes her cheeks while softly talking to her.

Suddenly her mother coughs and struggles to get up. With her right hand she pulls at the mask. When Peter removes it for her, she opens both her eyes and, after looking lovingly at her daughters, she turns to her husband, takes his hand and smiles. In a clear voice she says: "Peter."

She lays her head back on the pillow, takes one more deep breath and is gone.

Peter Dekker lays his head on his wife's chest and cries. Ann and Josie come around the bed to comfort their father and, holding each other close, they grieve with him.

It's hard to let her go and say their good-byes, but then Josie gets up and takes her father's hand.

"Come Papa, it's time to go."

"The two of you go ahead. I want to stay here with her, just a little longer."

FIVE

Carson, the children, and Tom and Catherine come to the Netherlands to attend the funeral; Ann is thankful to have her family with her, and their love gives her strength when they put her mother to rest. When everybody has left, she takes a walk by herself along the graves.

She needs a little time to herself and it's so peaceful here.

She finds her great grandparent's graves—*Jochem Bertus Jansen* and *Josephine Harmke Jansen Smid*.

Nearby are her grandparent's headstones. She traces their names, etched in the marble stone, with her finger—*Martin Jan Jansen* and *Anna Wilhelmina Jansen Gerritsma*.

She removes the dead flowers from the geraniums, which are planted in between the stones, and when she gets up, she notices Bas Boonstra's grave across the path. He's Bram's father; when he and his son came here from Haarlem, looking for food, during the horrible hunger winter of 1944, he died of sickness and starvation. The crude wooden cross, made by her Uncle Hank, is cemented in a white column.

"I can't remove the cross. It's like a part of him now," his wife Henrika told Ann's mother.

Ann walks past the graves of the Canadian soldiers who died here, fighting for the freedom of the Dutch. She stops and turns, and walks over to have a closer look.

The Canadian Maple Leaf, etched in the white glistening stones, bring tears to her eyes. She reads the names and where they were from. They were so young!

Near the entrance is a simple monument, dedicated to the men that lost their lives the day before the town was liberated, shot by a crazed German officer, right here on the other side of the graveyard's hedge. She recognizes their names on the plaque from the stories she heard so many times when growing up.

"I wondered where you were," Carson says. He takes her hand, puts his arm around her shoulder, and together they walk home.

A few days after the funeral, Peter Dekker asks his daughters to go through their mother's belongings. He keeps her wedding ring and the gold necklace he gave her on their wedding day. Some of her jewelry is given to Aunty Jenny, who still lives with Uncle Jan in the house down the street, which they purchased from Peter, when Uncle Jan retired. "The Bloch's House," they always call it.

The rest of her jewelry and keepsakes are divided between Ann and Josie.

In the bottom drawer of her mother's dresser, Ann finds a bundle of letters from Aunt Hanna, who moved to New York; and from there to Israel after the war. There is a dark brown braid of hair, wrapped in tissue paper, underneath the letters, and three notebooks, tied together with a red satin ribbon.

She recognizes her mother's handwriting.

Ann takes the notebooks and the braid downstairs and shows her father.

"I can't believe she still had these after all those years. She started writing, off and on, when she was twelve years old, I believe, and kept it up during the war. She started writing a book about that time, but when the two of you were born she left it alone; when you girls were old enough and your Ma went back to teaching, she abandoned it all together. Hmm—and this is Hanna's braid, isn't that something that all this is still here?"

"Would you mind if I read the books Pa, and perhaps finish her work? Is that okay?"

"I don't see any harm in that; sure, go ahead and read it, sweetheart."

She pours a glass of wine, settles into a comfortable chair and opens the first notebook. She cries often and laughs at some of her mother's entries. It's strange to find out things about her mother which she never knew, and to read about the life she had before Ann was born—and once was young too.

She feels closer to her now than ever before!

After a few days, when done with her reading, she asks her father to bike with her to the places her mother mentioned in the notebooks.

Just outside of town they stop and when they look back to the town, they see the church tower proudly keeping watch over the peaceful town below.

Just like Mamma wrote in her book, she thinks.

Her father stops at a fork in the road. He motioned her to follow him into the woods.

"Ah, here it is; this is where your mother and I put the supplies we took to the men in hiding, during the war," he says, pointing at a tree with the bottom of the trunk split by lightning.

"We'll take this narrow path to the sheepfold, the second hiding place."

Ann recognizes the path which leads to the sheepfold.

He lifts the lid of the well behind the shepherd's shed.

"And here we put the food for the other men. They were hiding over there, just a few minutes down this path. Now, let's take the regular path back to town."

They cross the road and follow the path toward the tower.

Her father stops and leans his bike against a huge old oak tree, called the 'Owl tree' by the town's people.

"This is where I kissed your mother for the first time; we never told you girls, did we?" he says and smiles.

"We went here on our first date. It's a long time ago, but it seems as if it was just yesterday."

Ann went to these parts of the forest so many times with her friends and family, and heard the stories, but never realizes how many fond and significant memories they held for her parents—until today.

"Let's go to the top of the tower. I never took you girls there, because it wasn't safe anymore, but it was restored a few years back. You can see for miles; it's a spectacular view."

It is beautiful. They sit down on the bench on the top floor and her father points to the little hamlets and towns in the distance.

"Look over there—a little to the left; you can see Uncle Hank's house from here!

This tower was built for the forest warden, a lookout to spot forest fires.

We used to call it "The Look-out". We went here often during our courtship and after we were married; before you girls came along, we used to take a basket with food up here, and stayed for hours. Your mother loved it."

"Did you read Ma's notebooks, Papa?"

"Yes I did, and I also read most of the book when she was working on it. Why?"

"Well, there are a few intimate details; would you mind if I mention those?"

"Your mother wrote it as it was, and although she didn't finish, I believe she would have wanted to share it with others. You go ahead, Annie, and try to keep it as authentic as you can, she would have liked that."

They stop for tea at Uncle Hank and Aunt Anneke's house. Uncle Hank renovated his grandparents' house, and he and Aunt Anneke raised their four children in the quaint little house, which sits at the edge of the forest.

Ann admires the shiny antique copper utensils that hang on a rack in Aunt Anneke's kitchen.

"Aren't they neat? And they have some history too!" Uncle Hank says.

"I found them when I was digging in the garden. Opa buried them during the war when the Germans collected metals to make ammunition. He apparently forgot where he had put them."

Ann enjoys her visit with her old Aunt and Uncle, and after she mentions her mother's notebooks, Uncle Hank and her father go back in time and recall their experiences during the war. Aunt Anneke clears the table, pours them each a cognac, and a cherry brandy for Ann and herself, and Uncle Jan and Pa light a cigar.

A few hours go by, and when they get up to leave, promises and plans are made to have a family dinner before Ann goes back home to Canada.

On the way back to town, she spots a patch of daisies in a field.

"Let's pick some of those pretty flowers, Papa."

She fills the basket with a big bouquet, and decides to stop at the cemetery, where she places the daisies on her mother's grave.

"I came to say good-bye for now, Mamma, and to tell you that I'm going to finish your book. I promise to tell it just the way you meant it to be told."

She stands by her mother's grave in thought for a few minutes. Then she and her father get back on the bicycles and ride home.

A few weeks later, when back in Canada, Ann sits down to read through her mother's notebooks one more time and, picking up where her mother left off, starts writing the rest of her mother's war memories book.

— 1936 to 1945 —

the LADYBUG RING

by Wilhelmina Jansen Dekker
Co-author, Anna J. Barlow Dekker.

CHAPTER 1

The Netherlands,
1936 – 1940.

It's a perfect day for a bicycle ride. The sun shines brightly and there's only a little bit of a breeze.

I pick up my friend Hanna, right after breakfast, and plan to pedal the path that goes all the way around town.

Hanna and I are like sisters. We grew up together and live on the same street, only a few houses apart. We started school together and are now in the fifth grade.

We don't look like sisters though—quite the opposite.

Hanna's hair is curly and dark brown, almost black, and she wears it into two long braids. Her eyes are hazel with golden specks, and her skin is a creamy olive color.

My hair is golden blond, and my eyes are leaf green.

"Emerald eyes," my mother always says.

I have freckles on my nose and cheeks. I don't like that, not at all! I wish to look like Hanna, so dainty and perfect! Hanna tells me she would like to look like me. "Mieneke, your hair is like spun gold, like the hair in Rapunzel's story" she says, every time she brushes it.

We love each other and are best friends.

We stop, before we go back to town, and, walking beside our bikes, we take the short cut across the field behind van Holt's farm to my grandparent's house.

"Let's have something to eat at Oma's. I'm hungry— you too?"

"Yes, I am. Do you think they're home?"

"They should be. They're always home at lunchtime."

I shield my eyes from the sun and look toward the house.

"I can see the laundry on the line from here."

"Do you miss going to your grandparent's house, Hanna?" I ask when we walk on.

"I wish I had grandparents to visit, but remember when I told you that Mamma's parents died a long time ago? And Opa and Oma Bloch died when I was very little. I don't remember them. Mamma's sister is old; she's like an Oma and she has many kids. I like to visit them, but it's so far away all the way to Scheveningen!"

"We can pretend Oma and Opa Jansen are your grandparents too. We're here now; we can ask them."

The small thatched-roof house, once home to the forest warden, is nestled against the edge of the woods. A narrow brick path leads to the front door. Beside the door an Azalea bush is in full bloom, displaying its splendid lavender flowers. A meticulously trimmed hedge surrounds the entire front yard, low growing conifers and evergreens cover the ground, painted throughout with the sunny colors of bright flowering annuals.

The area beside the house is laid in brick, all the way through to the back where a well sits in the corner. My Opa uses the pulley to hoist up the bucket filled with water for the garden.

Behind the house is a narrow strip of grass where the clothesline is. A holly hedge separates the back from a small potato field. A row of cages, for Opa's prized rabbits, sits against the wall of the chicken coop, where the chickens peck and scratch in the grassy dirt.

A small wooden gate opens into the vegetable garden, and berry bushes grow in a hedge all the way to the back. On the other side of the garden, apple and plum trees form a barrier between the street and the garden. Every year Opa plants vegetables, tomatoes and strawberries in straight neat rows.

Opa and Oma Jansen lived here for a long, long time. Uncle Jan and Papa grew up in this house, which Opa bought when he married my Oma, and that's more than fifty years ago! We had a big celebration for their fiftieth wedding anniversary. There were so many people there! All of my Opa and Oma's brothers and sisters came, with all their children and grandchildren. Most people from town came by too. Opa knows most people that live here. He used to deliver mail to every house.

He had more hair way back when, he always says. Now he shaves the little bit of hair that's left.

He looks so funny with his whole face and head covered in shaving cream. He shaves his head and his face at the same time! When I rub his head it's smooth and shiny.

Oma is in the back taking the laundry off the line. She puts the clothes pins in the pockets of her flowery apron. Her long white hair is braided and twisted in a bun on the nape of her neck. My Oma's name is Josephine Jansen. Opa and Oma have the same initials, Josephine and Jochem Jansen. I think it's pretty neat!

"That's why I married her," Opa says, but I don't believe him; he likes to joke a lot!

"What are you girls doing today? Oh my goodness me, look at your muddy socks—you came across that field again, didn't you? You'd better take them off; I'll give them a quick rinse. There's still wash water in the tub," Oma says and clicks her tongue.

"We went for such a long bike ride Oma, and we are so hungry! Can we have something to eat, please?"

"Well, that's good timing, girls—or did the smell of the soup I'm warming up—and the bread I just baked this morning—make you hungry?" says Oma.

"Mieneke, call Opa please—he's in the garden weeding the beans. He must be hungry too after all that hard work," she says and puts the last pins in her pocket.

"Do you need help carrying the wash in, Oma Jansen? I can carry the basket."

"Thank you, Hanna. Why don't we go inside and you can help set the table?"
Opa looks up when I call.

"Hi Opa; Oma wants you to come in. The soup is hot!"

"Hi Mieneke, my sweet girl," my Opa says. "What did you do with your socks?"
"Oh, never mind," he says, when he looks at my muddy clogs.

He smiles and takes my hand. "Let's have a bowl of Oma's delicious soup."

Opa has to bend his head to enter the porch through the low back door.

It's so clean and tidy inside.

The copper pump is spotless and polished to a high sheen, and wooden shoes are lined up, neatly in a row, against a whitewashed wall.

A bicycle rack is in the back beside the coal bin, and the door to the left leads to a small room with a wooden toilet. Opa cuts newspapers in neat squares for toilet paper, and hangs them on a nail beside the toilet.

The staircase in the far corner goes up to my grandparent's bedroom.

A two-burner gas stove, used for cooking in the warm summer months, sits on a small table beside the kitchen door.

The kitchen is small and cozy.

I like to watch my Oma when she polishes the big cooking stove. She puts the black polish on an old rag and wipes it all over the top. The lids of the stove are done separately and put on a sheet of newspaper. After the polish sits for a while, Oma takes crumpled up newspapers and, going around in circles, she polishes and polishes! Sometimes she gets so hot and has to wipe the loose hair strands off her forehead. Her dirty fingers leave big black streaks on her face, but she's not aware of it. It's so funny!

There are three holes in the top of the stove. Oma puts her pots on the holes when she cooks supper. She can also bake in the stove, and makes bread at least three times a week. In the winter Opa puts a few more logs in the stove and it keeps the whole house warm and cozy in the evening and through the night.

The only time we're allowed in the front room is on Sundays, birthdays and Holidays. Oma likes to keep the room nice.

There's a beautiful table in the middle of the room, with flowers and little leaves carved into the legs. The soft plush seats of the chairs are grey with dark green and purple stripes. There are two winged chairs by the windows, and shiny copper pots filled with flowering plants sit in every window sill.

A set of box beds, with pretty painted doors, is built along one wall. One of the beds is used for storage, but the other one still has a mattress and a cozy quilt. Hanna and I like to stay overnight at my grandparents. We're allowed to sleep in the box bed, and when we close the doors it's like sleeping in a big closet!

It smells so good in the kitchen. The aroma of vegetable soup and fresh-baked bread makes us even hungrier.

"Something smells good in here! How's my Hanna today? It's about time you come to see this old man!"

"Oh, Opa Jansen, you're not that old!"

Oma gets the dishes and ladles up the soup while Hanna slices and butters the bread, and I pour a glass of milk for Hanna and myself. Opa and Oma will have a cup of coffee.

"Quickly wash up, Opa—and Mieneke, can you move that chair please so we can all sit around the table?"

"Hanna doesn't have an Opa and Oma. Can you be her grandparents, too?" I ask, after we've all sat down.

"Would you like that, Hanna—or is it just Mieneke's idea?"

"I would like that, Oma Jansen."

"Well, I would like that too—and what do you think Opa?"

"It's a wonderful idea; why didn't we think of that sooner! I'd love to have another granddaughter! Come here and give your Opa a hug!"

Oma's vegetable soup always has tiny little meatballs in it. They taste so good! I eat mine first, but Hanna puts hers all around the edge of her plate and eats them last.

"Will you take us fishing by the canal later, Opa?" I ask.

"Not today girls. I'd better get those beans done, but tomorrow we can go. I'll dig up some fat worms for bait."

Our plates are empty and Opa fills his pipe. He leans back and smokes while visiting with us a little longer. The sweet pungent aroma of the tobacco fills the room, and white fluffy streams of smoke swirl up to the ceiling. Sometimes Opa blows rings and we try to poke our fingers through the middle.

Opa puts his pipe in the ashtray and gets up.

"I'd better finish the row of beans. See you both tomorrow girls—and wear your rubber boots!"

"Never mind the dishes," Oma says. "The two of you would probably like to get going. I'll tidy up. Before you go, put those loaves of bread in that bag, Mieneke. There's one for your Ma, too, Hanna. Now go straight home. No dillydallying!"

Around the corner from my grandparents' house, just before the road heads into town, we spot a patch of daisies along the ditch and spreading into the field.

"Let's pick flowers, Hanna!"

"Look, there's a little ladybug on this flower, I love ladybugs!"

Hanna carefully picks up the little bug and lets it walk along her finger, while singing,

"Ladybug, ladybug, fly away home
Your house is on fire
Your children all roam
Except little Nan
Who sits in her pan
Weaving as fast as she can."

She gently blows on the ladybug and it flies away.

We pick enough daisies to fill both of our baskets. "We'd better go home now. They're going to be so happy with the flowers!"

"Hey Ma, we picked flowers for you! And here's freshly-baked bread from Oma."

"Well, these flowers are so pretty! Get that big water jug from the shelf in the porch, Mieneke. That'll make for a nice vase, don't you agree? Are you hungry?"

"We ate already at Oma's house. We had soup, with little meatballs and bread."

"Are they both alright?"

"Yes, they're fine Ma. Opa was working in the garden. Can I go to Hanna's house and play a little longer? We have to take Vrouw Bloch her flowers too."

"As long as you're not underfoot and you're home in time for supper."

We skip along the cobblestone street to Hanna's house.

Almost out of breath, we reach Hanna's Pa's store.

As we open the door to the quaint little shop, we are greeted by the smell of old wooden cabinets, filled with rolls of fabric and neatly labeled boxes: Pins. Needles. Markers. Lace. Trims. Ribbons.

Scents of new woolens, silks and cottons are mingled with the smell of hot sewing machine oil.

Sam Bloch is measuring a man for a new suit. He's holding the thick stub of a pencil in the corner of his mouth and swings the measuring tape around the man's thick waist. The big man towers over him as he stands on the platform in front of the tailor, looking down on Sam's cap covered head. He has an intimidating glare in his eyes, and seems to be very important.

Sam looks up, and when he turns to write the measurements in his little green book, he nudges his head toward the kitchen door. We know very well to be quiet now and quickly walk through to the kitchen.

Minnie Bloch is a plump, short woman. She wears tiny little gold earrings and uses bright red lipstick on special occasions. She twists her long black hair in a knot on top of her head.

"Come in, girls, come in," Hanna's Ma, Minnie, says; she almost pulls us into the kitchen.

"I was just going to make some potato latkes; now you can help. Hanna, please put those nice daisies in a vase and put them on the table. Now, let me show you how to make the dough for the latkes."

Minnie puts a pan filled with oil on the stove to warm it up.

I'm not to call her Minnie of course; that's impolite. I have to say: "Meneer and Vrouw Bloch."

When the dough for the latkes is done, and the oil is hot enough, Vrouw Bloch fills a spoon with the batter, holds her hand about ten centimeters above the pan and, with a quick turn of her wrist, empties the spoon, all at once into the hot oil. "Splat!" She quickly pulls her hand back, so as not to burn herself.

We hover over the pan, and argue over the thinnest, crispiest little fritters, which are so thin you can almost see through them!

"Tsk, tsk," Hanna's Ma says; she says that often, and pushes us away from the hot pan. "Now sit down at the table and I will bring you some latkes while they're still nice and hot."

She takes two small plates, slides three latkes on each of them, and tops the fritters with a big dollop of applesauce. We hear the small brass bells above the shop's door chime. Minnie carefully opens the door, and when she sees that the important man has left, she calls her husband. "Sam dear, come have some latkes with the children."

Hanna's Pa comes into the kitchen and washes his hands by the sink.

"How are you girls today?" he asks when he sits down.

"I see you picked some pretty flowers for your Mamma."

Sam Bloch is a slight man, not nearly as tall as my father. His sideburns and beard are neatly trimmed, and he always wears a little black skullcap on his head. There are several pins stuck in his jacket's lapel, and the pencil stub is tucked behind his ear. With a twinkle in his eyes he listens to our chatter. He smiles once in a while and nods his head without saying much.

Vrouw Bloch serves him a bowl of chicken soup and a plate of latkes, but his are topped with heavy cream.

"Thank you, Minnie dear; they smell wonderful."

It's getting hot in the kitchen and Vrouw Bloch opens the windows wider. The pretty lace window screens, which Sam made himself, keep the bugs out.

A soft breeze now cools the room.

In Hanna's house the front room is called "The dining room."

Like it is at Oma's house, we're only allowed in the dining room on special days. Silver candlesticks, wine goblets, a tea set and a coffee urn, on its own little stand, are on display in a dark wood, tall buffet. Vrouw Bloch also has beautiful crystal glasses with a matching wine decanter, and a fancy gold-trimmed dinnerware set, which are used on special days.

The Blochs are Jewish and don't go to church on Sundays, but celebrate the Sabbath on Saturdays. They don't have Christmas or Easter either, but have Hanukah and other holidays. That's when the beautiful Menorah, which is a big candle holder, is used. When there's a celebration, the Menorah is placed in the middle of the dining room table and Meneer Bloch lights the candles.

Sometimes we're invited, and Minnie cooks special dishes and bakes beautiful breads for dinner.

My parents and the Blochs have been friends for many years. When Mamma was pregnant with me, the Blochs moved into their house—and Vrouw Bloch was pregnant too! And that's how they became friends.

We've eaten our latkes and go outside to play. There's a rope swing tied to the branch of a big oak tree in the courtyard behind Hanna's house. We take turns pushing each other. Higher...higher! Oh, it's like flying like a bird!

"Time to go home now Mieneke," Vrouw Bloch calls from the backdoor.

"It's almost dinnertime. Come in for a minute," she says. She wraps some latkes in a clean dishtowel for me to take home.

"Thank your Oma for the bread, please."

She puts some of the latkes on the back of the stove for Davie, Hanna's older brother.

My mother is peeling potatoes for supper. A bowl with the potatoes sits in her lap. She peels, hardly ever breaking the skin, quickly picks out the eyes, quarters the potato, and plops it in the pan with water in front of her on the table.

She's listening to the five o'clock news on the radio.

My mother, Anna Jansen, is tall and slim. She wears her long blond hair twisted in a roll and holds it together with a silver hairpin.

"She is the prettiest girl in town—that's why I married your Mamma," my father always says.

When my father came back to our town, after he went to school in Groningen, he started working at the dairy plant. My mother's father, Opa Gerritsma, worked there too, and was Papa's boss. When Opa retired, Papa got his job. Opa and Oma Gerritsma moved into a smaller place, and Papa bought their house. Opa and Oma Gerritsma are dead now. First Opa died, and then Oma had to go into a home, because she forgot who she was and also didn't recognize us. Then, a few years after Opa had passed away, she died too. I was only five years old when that happened and I don't remember them much.

Hank, my brother, was born in this house first, and I came three and a half years later. I think we will always live here.

"Here are some latkes from Vrouw Bloch Mamma."

"Oh, dear Minnie spoiled us again! I'll warm them up later and we can have them for dessert. Now, you finish your ten rows of knitting, and then set the table please Mieneke."

"I don't want to knit right now!"

"Come now, busy hands are happy hands, Mieneke!"

Opa and Oma Jansen's house was built many, many years ago.

Our house is newer and modern.

Ma papered the walls in pretty colors that match the white and green tiled floor. The kitchen cupboards are painted pastel green with white accents and knobs, and Pa put a long rod above the stove for ladles, spoons and other kitchen utensils.

A cute frilly curtain hangs in the window.

"The heart of our home,"—that's what my mother always says—is the big oak kitchen table, around which we have our meals, read, play cards and do jig-saw puzzles.

The front room is separated from the kitchen by stained glass sliding doors. There are four comfortable chairs around the large coffee table.

Pa's smoking table, with his collection of pipes and cigarette holders, is beside the green plush sofa in front of the bay windows. The windowsills hold all of Ma's pretty houseplants.

A large, beautifully carved mahogany cabinet is filled with fancy dishes, the tea set, which is decorated with little roses, and all the crystal.

I love the cute lotion bottles, which are Ma's birthday gifts from Vrouw Bloch. Ma lined them all up in the cabinet, but never opened a bottle.

"They're just too pretty," she always says.

The bottom drawers of the cabinet hold Ma's keepsakes and all the good linen.

A brick fireplace heats the room, and the big chimney also warms the upstairs where Hank and I sleep.

Wallpaper with gold and red velvety flowers matches nicely with the sunny yellow painted window and door frames. I know the color is called "Sunny Yellow", because it said so on the can when Ma and I picked it out at the paint store.

The kitchen is heated by the big boiler in the porch. Pa explained to me how it circulates hot water to the kitchen, the bathroom and the radiator in the hall.

The bathroom is by the stairs at the end of the long hall across from my parents' bedroom.

Beside the garage, a small gate opens on a tiled path leading to a brick patio, on which wicker garden furniture sits, surrounded by roses and lilac bushes.

Papa built a pond where our sand box used to be. He even built a small bridge across the water, and Hanna and I like to sit there in the sun, with our feet dangling in the water, and we watch the goldfish swim around and hide underneath the water plants and rocks.

A long hedge comes all the way from the street to the back and separates the gravel path beside our house from the vegetable garden.

My father comes home from work at six o'clock. He hangs his coat on the wooden peg by the kitchen door, washes up at the sink in the porch and slips off his clogs before he steps into the kitchen.

Martin Jansen, my Pa, is a tall man. His dark auburn hair is cut short in a taper. "Taper it again, please," I hear him say to the barber, when he takes me along to the barbershop.

I like it when Papa takes me along for his haircuts.

Old men sit and visit around the potbelly stove, and smoke their pipes and cigars.

On the wall are two large colorful advertisement of a pipe tobacco brand called "Comfort". I can't take my eyes of the picture with a man who is put in a pillory, which sits on a platform in the middle of a town's square, and I wonder what he's been punished for. People jeer and throw rotten tomatoes at him, but on the picture beside it, one man steps up and offers the captured man a drag of his pipe, filled with Comfort tobacco. I'm glad that at least one person in the crowd is kind.

When the barber has finished Pa's haircut, he combs the hair back and holds it in place with nice smelling hair cream, and before we leave, the barber hands me half a dozen butterbeans—a real treat since we don't have candies often.

I look at Pa's new haircut and think that he's very handsome.

"Hi Papa," I say, when he comes through the door, and give him a hug.

"How's my big girl today." He kisses the top of my head.

"I smell kale-hotchpot and bacon, my favorite meal, and I'm hungry!"

He lifts the lid of the pan, but before he can even have a peek, Ma playfully taps his fingers with a wooden spoon. "Wait for supper, Martin! Can I warm up a cup of coffee for you? And here is today's newspaper."

Pa settles himself in his comfortable chair with his coffee and the paper, and I set the table. One plate I set aside for Hank, who will be home a little later.

Hank, my brother, is going to be a mechanic, and attends trade school in the city.

Outside the wind is picking up and it starts to rain. When Ma is just about to close the window, we hear Hank's bike through the gravel.

"You're home early, son. I thought you had an extra class today."

"Pa, you forgot already? We have to go to the Scout's Jamboree meeting tonight!"

"Oh dear, I did forget! Can we eat right away, Ma? We can't be late!"

I help Ma with the dishes and after we've tidied up the kitchen, I take my library book and curl up in Papa's chair. I had better finish it—it's due tomorrow.

"Do you remember that it's Hanna's birthday the day after tomorrow, Ma?"

"Yes, I know, Mieneke. You'll have to come home right after school, and we'll bake a cake."

"Can I decorate the cake please?"

"Yes, you can, and I'll pick some flowers from the garden for Minnie's table, but now it's time for bed, Mieneke—it's almost nine. We'll talk about Hanna's birthday tomorrow."

I kiss my mother goodnight and go upstairs to the loft. We don't have bedrooms upstairs, but Pa cornered off a space for me along the staircase. I like my "bedroom". I have my own wardrobe, a mirrored dresser in one corner and a chest at the back of my bed. I store all my keepsakes—which I collected since I was little—in that chest. A cozy quilt, which Oma made me for my tenth birthday, tops the bed.

Hank's corner is around the chimney by the window. His collection of fossils is on display in the windowsill. There are lots of little sea urchins, shells and rocks, embedded with tiny shells, leaves and insects. He has a mammoth tooth, a disk of a reindeer, a tiny jaw of a vole, and one of an otter.

He proudly explains every new find to me:

"These are millions of years old, Mieneke."

His model construction kit sits on his night table, but he never plays with it anymore.

I'm not supposed to, but I leave the light on. I want to read the last few pages of my book.

I hear Hank and my father come home, and shortly after Hank comes upstairs and turns off the light.

"Goodnight Hank," I call to him.

"Oh, you're still awake, Sis? Goodnight!"

I can hear my parents talking downstairs, but I can't make out what they're saying. The clock of the big church, just around the corner, strikes ten, and I drift off to sleep.

Ma gives me some money for Hanna's birthday gift the following day, and I go to the variety store. There is so much to choose from! I see a doll that looks like a real baby. Hanna would like that, but maybe we're too old for dolls now.

I decide to look around a little longer.

I walk up three wooden steps toward the glass showcases in front of the cash register. The cases are filled with jewelry, bows and hairpins, combs and brushes, bow-ties, wallets, tie clips and one with cigarette holders, pipes and silver matchbox holders. I look through all of them, and then go back to the jewelry case. I follow my finger over the glass, from right to left and back again.

I trace all the rows, and then I see it. The perfect gift for Hanna! A silver ring with a red stone shaped like a Ladybug. It even has tiny black dots on its wings!

The lady behind the counter puts it in a small silver-colored ring box and wraps it in pretty paper.

I leave home a little earlier on the morning of Hanna's birthday. I'm anxious to see if she likes her birthday present. Hanna looks so sweet in her best Sunday dress and she has a freshly-starched ribbon in each of her braids.

"Happy birthday, Hanna—here is your present!"

Hanna loves the ladybug ring and it fits her finger perfectly!

Vrouw Bloch hands Hanna a cookie tin filled with red candies that look like raspberries. Hanna's Ma says she counted them twice to make sure there are two candies for each of our classmates.

It's a nice sunny walk to school. We rattle a stick along the fence of Willem's farm and sing, "Ladybug, ladybug…"

The smell of freshly-baked bread wafts through the open door of the bakery, and Vrouw Drost waves at us from behind the butcher's shop window.

We cross the playground by the old gym and go through the gates of our school. Children put their bikes away in the racks, and a few boys play a quick game of marbles before the school bell rings.

The big doors swing open. Meneer Vos, the third grade teacher, makes sure all the kids are properly lined up in an orderly fashion before they enter the school's hall.

"Happy birthday, Hanna," he says when he sees her in the row.

"Thank you Meneer Vos," Hanna says, and blushes a little bit.

"We have a birthday today," our teacher says, after all the children sit at their desks. Hanna is called to the front of the class, where, with a shy smile, she stands beside the blackboard. We all sing "Happy birthday", and then she walks through all the rows to hand out her raspberry candies.

The table in Minnie's dining room is set so fancy. Two silver candlesticks and Ma's pretty flowers sit in the middle of the table. Beside each gold-rimmed plate is a real crystal glass, even for the children. Hanna and I cut the five pointed starred paper coasters for underneath each glass.

"It's hard to believe our girls are already twelve, Minnie. It seems as if it was only yesterday that they were little babies," Ma says.

Sam, Minnie and Davie sing a song for Hanna in Hebrew:

"Yom huledet Same'ach, Hayom yom huledet, Hanna," and then we all sing happy birthday in Dutch.

Meneer Bloch fills the glasses with sweet red wine, and pours red berry juice with a few drops of the wine in the children's glass.

Vrouw Bloch serves her delicious roasted chicken and vegetables. There are also potato kugels, fishcakes and pretty braided loafs of bread.

We all have a big piece of the birthday cake that Mamma and I baked, for dessert.

When it's time to go, Papa says, "You have to roll me home Anna; I'm too full to walk!"

I'm allowed to stay. We always stay at each other's house for a sleep over on our birthdays.

"Which boy in our class do you like the best, Hanna?"

"I like Harm Oostra; he is so nice and I like his brown eyes. He's so good-looking, don't you think? Who do you like the best?"

"I like Peter Dekker. Yes… I like him the best…hmmm…maybe Frans Tolsma. I like him a lot, too."

"When we get married one day, I'll live in our house and you live in your house. We will still be neighbors, and our children can be friends like us."

"Yes, but first we have to have a period or else we won't have children."

"A period? Why? And what *is* a period?"

"My Ma says we have little eggs inside of us and once a month there's a period when they have to come out. It bleeds a little bit, but my Ma said not to be scared—it doesn't hurt. It's just a nuisance and I should tell her right away when it happens.

We need a period to have children. We have to be married too."

"When will this happen do you think?"

"Well, we're twelve, and that's why Ma told me. It could happen any day now, It's strange."

"Yes, it's very strange, and I don't think I would want it. Good night, Hanna."

"Me neither; I don't like it at all. Good night, Mieneke."

We finish grade six, two months after our birthdays, and school is out for the summer. We will not return to the elementary school in our town.

After our vacation, my friends and I will attend the high school in the city.

Hanna and I pick up the school supply list and read it over and over again. The next day we go to the city to do our shopping.

"I never bought my own school supplies," Hanna says.

"Me neither—it's so exciting!"

When all our shopping is done, and we've put it all away in our brand new school bags, Hanna says, "I'm hungry, and I have enough money left to buy something to eat. Do you want to go to the fish stand?"

"Yes, that would be nice. I'm hungry too, and I have enough money left to buy a few salt herrings to take home. Hank will like that!"

Meneer Bloch sews our new summer coats and they're ready for our first school day. The coats are identical, made from light blue gabardine with dark blue corduroy collars and sleeve cuffs. Hanna's father covers the buttons with the corduroy material to match.

Oma knits two pairs of lacy ankle socks for each of us. "You're both too old now for knee-high socks," she says, and Mother takes us to the store in the city to buy new shoes.

We're excited and feel very special when we get ready for high school on the first morning.

With four other teenagers, we bike the twenty minutes to the city every school day.

Between the canal and the road is a narrow bike path, just wide enough for two bikes riding side by side. The road is sparsely lined with tall skinny trees. There are farms every kilometer or so apart along both sides of the canal. Houses, a store and a café are clustered together by the bridges, and small villages line both sides of the highway.

Hanna and I ride together every day. We sing songs, do riddles, and practice the French words we need to remember for next day's lesson.

We're goofy at times, and pull and push each other in the wind.

Peter Dekker, the son of the principal of our elementary school, and Peer Winters, whose father has a farm just out of town, cycle together. They always talk politics and are so serious!

Margie Tiemen, a shy little girl, is pushed along by her big brother Tom. He's very protective of his little sister after their father died last year of pneumonia.

Hanna and I spend a lot of time together. We like to go shopping, play basketball, take music lessons, and we go for long walks and bicycle rides in the forest. One Saturday afternoon each month we go to the tennis court by the pavilion for lessons.

"They are joined together at the hips," Hank always says. He likes to tease us a lot!

We have to study real hard to make the grades we need for university. We both want to be teachers. We will work in the same city and in the same school, and we'll room together. We've planned it all, and we're sticking to it!

CHAPTER 2

It's a splendid afternoon in the early spring of 1940, and Hank and Peter Dekker came along for a long bike ride in the forest. We rest on the edge of a ditch, with our feet dangling just above the still murky water.

The yellow old grass smells musky and feels damp, but young green blades are poking through, promising an early summer.

Across a freshly-ploughed field, our picturesque town basks in the afternoon sun. The church's silvery spire proudly keeps watch over the red-roofed dwellings, neatly plotted gardens and farmer's fields. Foliage in shades of green is dotted throughout as if thoughtfully painted there. The mill's bright white sails, contrasted against the stark blue sky, command the squinting of our eyes.

We sit back, resting on our elbows, our faces turned to the already warming sun.

Hank and Peter are talking politics.

"There's going to be trouble," Peter says. "Did you read the newspapers? My father and I listened to that guy Hitler on the radio the other day. He sounded like a fanatic. He's all fired up! My Pa says he's dangerous. He and his Party are gaining way too much power. They already annexed Austria, and then took a large part of Czechoslovakia, and kicked those poor Czechs out of their own homes. 'Czechoslovakia has ceased to exist,' that lunatic Hitler said in one of his rambling loud speeches. Then, in September last year, they took Poland.

Great Britain and France are the only countries who took action and declared war on Germany. They keep a close eye on Hitler, but that won't stop him. There's going to be trouble!"

We all sit up.

"But there's no fighting now, Peter, and if we stay neutral again, together with Belgium and Luxemburg, we should be okay, I think," Hank says.

"This is just the calm before the storm, my father said," says Peter. He gets up, walks over to our bikes, and asks, "Are there any sandwiches left in your basket Hanna?"

"Are you scared, Mieneke? Do you believe there will be a war?" Hanna asks on the way home.

"I don't know, I've never paid much attention to the news; but don't worry, Hank is very smart, and he said that the Netherlands most likely won't get involved."

"I hope he's right; Papa was born in Germany—he moved here with his parents when he was still a baby, but people might know and not like him because he is from there. That's what worries me a little."

"Hanna, people here don't think like that; they don't care where one is from. Besides, everybody likes your parents and nobody would hate your Pa because he was born in Germany! Honestly, you're so silly sometimes!"

It's my fourteenth birthday today, and although it's not a school day, I get up early.

The smells of bacon and pancakes, my favorite breakfast, make me rush down the stairs.

"Good morning, birthday girl. Wait a minute now, don't sit down yet!"

Hank blindfolds me with a tea towel and guides me, carefully avoiding any obstacles in my way, to the porch. My parents are right behind us. My father removes the towel and they all yell: "Happy Birthday!"

I look at a shiny bike. Its handle is adorned with a bright red ribbon.

"We hope you like your present, Mieneke," Pa says. "Hank fixed and polished the bike in his free time."

"Let me explain the gear system and the brakes to you, Sis. It's a little different than your old bike; it's taller and you won't touch the handlebar with your knees anymore! Let's take it outside and you can go for a spin," Hank says with a happy grin.

I give my family a big hug and take my new bike around the block.

In the evening, the Blochs come over for supper. Hanna brings a basket, neatly wrapped in the tailor's shop wrapping paper, for my new bike.

Oma and Opa come too. Oma knitted me a scarf and toque from the softest wool.

"I knitted the scarf and Oma knitted the toque," Opa says.

"Oh dear me, don't listen to him. If you knitted anything at all, then I'm the Queen of China," Oma says. "See what I have to put up with? We hope you like your present, Mieneke."

"She's spoiled rotten!" Hank says.

My birthday comes to a perfect end, with Hanna staying for the night. We laugh and giggle until Father yells at the bottom of the stairs: "Lights out!"

Peter was right. The Germans unexpectedly invade the Netherlands on May 10, 1940. The ill-prepared Dutch army resists and fights a tough battle. Many lose their lives, more are injured and, after five days of heavy battle, the Netherlands falls to the Germans. After heavy bombing destroys the city of Rotterdam and kills thousands of its people, the Dutch capitulate.

It's still early in the morning and Ma and I are sowing vegetable seeds in the just tilled soil, when we hear rumbling sounds in the distance. Somebody yells, "It's the Germans. The Nazis have invaded us! We're at war! The Germans are here!"

We look at each other in shock, drop the seeds and run to the street. People have already gathered on the corner. Pa is there and we run over to him.

"What's going on, Martin? Is it really the Germans?" Ma asks.

"Yes, I was told they're on the other side of the canal. A few of our men plan to blow up the bridge!' Pa whispers.

Most of us are worried; some people are scared, but others are just curious. Suddenly the booming sound of an explosion shakes the ground and rattles the windows. Mothers grab their children and herd them inside. Men grab whatever they can get their hands on—hunting guns, pitchforks, shovels and axes. Some even hold fence posts.

Another explosion spooks a farmer's horse. He throws his head back and bolts. The wagon hits the back of the frightened animal and it races off at top speed through the street. People quickly jump out of his path and several barely escape being run over. The wagon, filled with manure, bangs uncontrollably behind the scared animal. When coming around a corner, the wagon crashes into a row of milk cans, spilling milk all over the road. The noise of the banging cans scares the horse even more. The farmer hangs onto the reins with all his might, and desperately tries to get his horse under control. When the back of the wagon slams into a light pole, the driver is ejected from his seat and falls to the street.

One man tries to stop the horse. He jumps in its path and, waving his arms, he yells, "Whoa, whoa," but it keeps running. The wagon almost tips and spills half of its load. The man is covered in manure and narrowly escapes the wild galloping beast. The horse finally slows down when the wagon loses a wheel and tips over into the ditch. Somebody gets hold of the reins and, using all his strength, manages to bring the horse to a stop.

His rippling coat is steaming from sweat, and his eyes roll wildly in his head. The farmer calms it down and ties it up to a fencepost before he has a look at the damage. The spilled manure causes a horrible stench, but with some helping hands the mess is quickly cleaned up.

The sky above the canal is black with billowing clouds of smoke, but the explosions have stopped. Are the Germans coming our way? And what will they do once they get here?

Some houses near the bridge are damaged, and a few people sustain minor injuries. Jan, father's brother, who's the operator at the locks, lives in one of the houses closest to the bridge.

"I'd better go and check on Uncle Jan. Go inside with your mother, Mieneke, and wait for me there. I shouldn't be too long," my father says.

After an hour or so, Pa returns with my Uncle Jan and his wife Aunt Jenny. Pa pushes the handcart filled with their valuables and some clothes. Aunt Jenny is still in shock. They both have cuts and bruises from fallen debris. "Instead of telling Jenny to wait it out in the cellar, I should have send her to stay with you."says Uncle Jan.

The next day Uncle Jan and father check the house.

"The damage is worse than I first thought," Uncle Jan says. "Windows are blasted out, and the front door doesn't close properly, and a few bricks from the chimney tumbled down. We're boarded up for now, but we need a bed for a few days Anna, if that's okay with you. I'll start with the repairs tomorrow during work hours."

Ma and Aunt Jenny set up a makeshift bed in the front room, and their belongings are put upstairs, for the time being.

The Germans repair the bridge and come marching through town in droves. Long columns of army trucks, jeeps and big tanks lead the rows and rows of soldiers on bicycle, horse and on foot.

Above all the noise I can hear the intimidating, clicking, stomping sounds of the soldiers' heavy cleated boots. Officers, in fancy uniforms, sit high and proud in their cars, shouting orders as they drive back and forth along the moving troops.

Thank God there's no fighting in our town, and only a handful of the soldiers and a few officers stay. They settle in and set up office in one of the hotels, owned by a N.S.B. member, a Nazi collaborator. The others keep marching to the next towns and cities, confiscating large estates, government buildings and hotels on their way, until they're spread all over the Netherlands.

Princess Juliana and the little princesses leave the Netherlands, and shortly thereafter, Queen Wilhelmina and her government go into exile in England.

I have many questions. Why did they leave? What will happen to our country without our Royal family here with us? When will they be back, and where did the princesses go? Some rumors say they went to Canada—is that true? Who will look after the palaces? Certainly Prince Bernard, who is married to Juliana, and is a German himself, can speak to the German authorities.

Uncle Jan and father repair the house by the canal and, after one month of sleeping on the floor in our front room, Aunt Jenny and Uncle Jan are happy to move back home.

Life as we know it goes on pretty much the same as before the war.

Why, I wonder, are the Germans even in our town? They act superior for sure, but they don't bother anybody much.

However, changes do come little by little. A few of Hank's friends quit the Scouts and join the Youth Storm, a Nazi collaborating youth club. When Hank refuses to become a member, they cut all ties with him and his remaining friends.

Dutch collaborators want their children to stay with their own kind. Jews and Jehovah Witnesses are shunned and bullied, and soon the young collaborators form boisterous and pompously behaving cliques.

Bigger and worse changes happen in the following year. Jews working in government are dismissed. Jewish lawyers, doctors, journalists, teacher and other Jewish professionals are fired or shut down. Christians are forbidden to do business with Jews, and stores owned by Jews are closed. Their cars, radios, bicycles and valuables are confiscated for "the good of the war effort".

Our Mayor is ousted and replaced by a new Mayor, who is a member of the N.S.B., of course! I recognize the new Mayor! He's the man I saw being measured for a new suit in Sam Bloch's shop before the war!

"The N.S.B. is worse than the Nazis. They will betray their own family, friends and neighbors. They believe they're so mighty and powerful. They have no shame, and do whatever it takes to put themselves in a good light with the Germans, to make sure their possessions and their careers are secured and to save their own ass! They're cowards and traitors, and not to be trusted, ever!" I overhear my father say.

Hanna is not allowed to go to our school anymore. She has to attend a school for Jews only, but when her bike is taken away, and she's not allowed to ride the bus, she has to stay home every day. We're not allowed to visit, not even in our own backyards, and Hanna looks so sad when, from behind her dining room window, she sees me leave for school in the morning.

All the Jews have a curfew now and have to stay inside from dusk till dawn. They also have to sew a yellow star, the Star of David, on their garments. "Jew" it says, so everybody knows they're Jews. Why? I don't understand any of these horrible new rules and it makes me so sad. I miss Hanna so much and cry myself to sleep almost every night.

Peter Dekker, who now rides beside me most school days, explains that the Germans don't like the Jewish people. They don't like Gypsies, Blacks, Jehovah Witnesses or anybody else who doesn't share their beliefs or who have a lifestyle that's not agreeable with what the Nazis believe is the proper way to live.

Only people of the pure German, Aryan race are desirable. They should be tall, fair, blue-eyed and strong. Hitler's, "Master Race!"

"Poor Hanna, what will happen to her and others like her, Peter?"

"It's too early to tell, Mieneke. Hopefully this will all come to a quick end. It's ridiculous, really, that it's even going on!"

When we get to the city, I see a long row of people, all wearing the yellow star, being escorted to the train station by black-uniformed SS Nazis. It makes me feel very uncomfortable and I worry about Hanna and her family. Will they be taken too? And where are all these people going?

"Will I ever be able to visit with Hanna again?" I ask my mother that afternoon.

"Oh, Mieneke, for sure; we'll find a way. I'll talk to your father when he comes home and we'll see what we can do. This war can't last; it'll be over soon and everything will be back to normal again!"

"I'll talk to Sam after supper tonight, but no word to anyone, Mieneke. We have to keep it a secret!" Pa says.

He brings Hanna to our house that same evening. It's the first sleepover since curfew began, and we have a lot of catching up to do!

"I don't understand what's happening, Mieneke. Papa said not to worry, but I'm scared. Why do the Nazis single us out? Why the Jews? Do you remember when I told you that I was worried about the Dutch not liking Papa, because he was born in Germany? You said how silly I was, and you were right; it's not the Dutch I should worry about, but the Germans, and it's because we're Jewish! My parents never got involved in any politics, nor did they ever commit a crime—and they're always so kind to everybody. Why can't I go to school? What difference does it make that I'm Jewish, or that one is of a Christian faith, or any other religion for that matter? We're all people!"

"Peter told me it's not only the Jews that are not liked by the Germans. Please don't worry, Hanna. Everybody says this war won't last."

I repeat what Peter told me, but I don't tell her about the row of Jewish people I saw at the train station.

We visit a few times each week, and sometimes Davie, who is home from college now, comes too. If he and Hank aren't visiting, Davie helps us with our English and Math, and we go over my other homework, so Hanna won't fall too far behind. Davie looks so much older with his new glasses. I really like him and have a little crush on him! I keep my mouth shut of course; Hank would tease me relentlessly!

Life is not getting any easier. We're allotted food stamps and have coupons for everything! For food, clothing, shoes, fuel, gasoline. There's nothing one can buy without these coupons, except for what's available on the black market for a ridiculously high price!

The Nazis figure out all kind of ways to keep the Dutch population under their control. Only persons that are registered will be given the coupons; others have to go without food or supplies.

"It's a way for the Germans to find out where everybody lives, and that way they're able to seek out the Jews and other 'undesirables,'" Peter tells me.

Loads and loads of food are trucked from Dutch warehouses to Germany to feed their army and the German people. The allotment of stamps is getting more limited each month. Sugar, cheese, milk and butter are now luxuries, and coffee is replaced with horrible tasting "stamp coffee".

It's illegal to butcher one's own cattle, pigs and other livestock, without reporting it to the authorities, so all the meat can be distributed legally.

Luckily, there are canned fruits, vegetables, pickled meat, dried fish and last year's apples left in the cellar.

"And we always have the garden," Ma says.

CHAPTER 3

January 1942 – December 1943

The streets are deserted in the evenings. People stay inside.

Everybody has a curfew and nobody, without a good reason, is allowed to be out in the streets after eight p.m.

Pa fabricates a good reason! He hires Hank and applies for a pass for each of them. They have to be able to go to the dairy plant if there's a mechanical problem with the system. Now, when they're out at night for any other reason, they have an excuse.

"We had a problem at the plant," they say, when stopped and questioned.

"We needed to do some repairs."

There seem to be problems at the plant quite often. Hank and Pa are out many nights and don't come home until the early morning hours.

Nobody tells me anything, but I know. I read the paper and listen to the illegal radio, when nobody's paying any attention to me.

I say nothing.

I know about the secret room they built back in the coal room. The room is big enough for a few chairs and a small table, on which the illegal radio and a map sit. The narrow door is hidden behind a shelving unit stacked with Pa's tools, flowerpots and boxes with old newspapers. The whole unit slides to the left to reveal a narrow opening leading into this secret meeting room. I know they listen to the English radio and messages from the Queen on "Radio Orange".

I need to find out what they're doing, and one evening I decide to go up to the small loft above the porch.

I sneak up the ladder, and my heart nearly stops when I step on a creaky step, I freeze, and stand very still for a few second before I move on. I slide on my stomach over the dusty wooden floor to a hole in the far corner. The hole is big enough to see Pa and Hank's heads, bent over the map or listening to the radio.

I'm as quiet as a mouse, barely breathing. I know I'll be in a lot of trouble if they find me here, but I want to know what's going on. I need to know!

There are three other men in the room tonight. One of them is Paul de Wal, the baker. Cor Dekker, Peter's father, is there too. And then I see Peter! Peter? What is he doing here, and why is he keeping secrets from me? He's supposed to be my friend! I put my ear closer to the hole. I need to know what they're talking about.

"I can still supply the bread, and I know that Drost the butcher still can help with meat, but not for very much longer he said. We have to get our hands on those food stamps as soon as possible, and I'm afraid we have to go to the city again to stock up. The shelves in the stores here are sparsely stocked. Chickens, pigs and even the vegetables from the gardens are taken by the Germans on a regular basis. It gets harder to feed the people in hiding."

"We're expecting a shipment any day now," Pa says. "We were promised a few I.D. cards too."

"Well, they better hurry up!"

They're whispering now and I can barely hear them.

I almost stop breathing when I hear Sam Bloch's name mentioned.

"Have you talked to Sam Bloch, Martin?" Peter's father asks. "Time is running out. Too many Jews have been rounded up. We have to get them out now! We found a safe place, but we can't wait any longer, we have to hurry before it's too late!"

I clasp my hand over my mouth to stifle a gasp.

It's too late for what? What are they talking about?

I slide down the ladder in a hurry, and almost forget the creaky step. I'm shaky now and my stomach feels queasy. I brush the dust of my clothes and quickly throw a handful of cold water in my face. I make it into the kitchen just in time. As soon as I sit down at the table, I hear the men leaving through the back door. Peter and his Pa leave first. Paul de Wal lingers for a few minutes, and then he too rushes off.

It's almost eight o'clock.

Ma comes into the kitchen from her bedroom. Hank goes upstairs to get his book and I put the kettle on.

"Keep a few cups of brew for us, Mieneke," Pa says. "We'll be back in fifteen minutes, Anna dear. Are you coming Hank?"

I know, without a doubt, that they're sneaking through the back gardens to the Bloch's house.

I don't sleep very well that night. I toss and turn. I sleep a little, but then I startle and I'm awake again. I'm so worried and frightened for Hanna. I'll have to talk to Peter first thing in the morning. He had better tell me what's going on! Why aren't they talking to me? Hanna is my best friend!

It's Ma's birthday today. There's a special breakfast of fresh bread, eggs, cheese and real coffee! I can't rush off, not yet! As soon as the dishes are done, I'll tell Ma I have to go to Peter to get a school book.

Peter's house is beside the elementary school. The house is surrounded by a beautiful flower garden. I lean my bike against a big willow tree and walk up the path to the front door, but when I'm just about to ring the doorbell, Peter comes around the corner. "Mieneke, what a surprise to see you here," he says, but when he comes closer and sees my face he says, "Holy, you look pissed!"

"I *am* pissed, you're right! I'm damn furious! What's going on Peter? Tell me what's happening to the Blochs?"

"Whoa, what the hell? What are you talking about?"

He grabs my arm and quickly pulls me behind the garden shed.

"I spied on you when you were at my house last night and I heard what was said. Now, tell me Peter, what's going on? I thought you were my friend and I could trust you. I don't understand it; Hanna is your friend too!"

"Mieneke, I'm sorry, but I can't tell you anything. The others trust me, and if I talk, even to you, they'll never trust me again! Go home and talk to your father, and after you've done that, you and I can talk tomorrow. Please, you'll have to take my word for it. I can't tell you."

"Is that you, Mieneke? Would the two of you like something to drink?" Vrouw Dekker asks as she steps out on the back veranda.

"Not today, Vrouw Dekker, but thank you. Its Ma's birthday and I promised to be right back. We will talk tomorrow, Peter?"

"We will if I can, and please don't take it personally, okay?"

I'm nervous on the way home, but I have no choice. I have to talk to my father. He'll be so mad at me!

Pa is reading his book in the front room. Thank God he's alone!

"Hi Pa, can I talk to you please?"

"Sure; what would you like to talk about?"

"Please Father, don't be mad at me, but I have listened to the meetings. I would like you to tell me what's going to happen to the Blochs. What about Hanna? Where are they going, Pa? I'm so worried!"

My father slowly closes his book, puts it on the table and walks over to the window. With his back turned to me, and anger in his voice, he says, "You have *what*? Oh, Mieneke—how could you be so sneaky! Have you talked to anybody else about this? Please, tell me you haven't! This is not good, not good at all!"

"I talked to Peter, but he doesn't want to tell me anything. He said I should talk to you. I'm so sorry, Father, but nobody ever tells me what's going on. I'm seventeen years old. I'm not a baby anymore! Hanna is my friend, I'm worried and I should be told!"

Slowly my father turns around. "I know you're almost an adult—and that's what worries me—you shouldn't have been so deceitful. You should have talked to me sooner!"

"And would you have told me then, Pa? Would you have told me anything, if I hadn't found out about it first?"

"No, I guess you're right. I probably wouldn't have, but you're my little girl! I tried to protect you, but you're right. I'll have to come to terms with the fact that you're growing up. Sit down, and we will talk."

"It's very bad all over Europe. The Germans are ruthless, and do whatever it takes to invade and conquer countries all over the world. Cities are bombed to smithereens, and thousands of our people have died. People are suppressed, and their rights are taken away. If the Nazis suspect anybody of having done anything against the German regime, they're arrested, questioned, often tortured and imprisoned in a slave work camp, or they're murdered without a trial."

"Young men are ordered to report to the German authorities and send to work-camps."

"Can they do that Pa? There are laws, even during a war, aren't there?"

"Yes, you're right. There are international laws, but laws mean nothing if they're not observed, and the Germans ignore the law and act like absolute criminals! The Jews are rounded up and taken away. The ones from around here are taken to a camp in Westerbork. We don't know where they go from there, but we expect it's not a very nice place. We have to get the Blochs out of here, as soon as possible. We have found a safe place, but Sam Bloch was so reluctant to go. He's too naïve and can't believe this is really happening, but we finally convinced him last night that it's time. One of our guides will pick them up from our house tomorrow night and take them to their hiding place, and hopefully to England, if we can make that happen."

"Our food and supplies are rationed, as you know," he continues. "We're forbidden to have meetings, listen to the radio or print newspapers. If we speak out against the Nazi party or do anything 'illegal', the Germans will kill us. Heaven forbid if they found the radio—it could cost us our lives. Remember when you asked about our car, and I told you I'd sold it? Well, I lied. I hid it over at Herman Winters' farm, and if I had not done that, the Germans would have confiscated it."

Dad takes a deep breath: "Men are ordered to report to the German authorities and then are deported to the work-camps."

He adds, "We have to be so careful, not only because of the Germans, but because of the traitors among us. The N.S.B party members are more dangerous and fanatical than the Nazis. Although some of them have regrets now and wished they had never joined, others are overjoyed to be part of the German occupation. We are the lucky ones. We have enough food and vegetables from the garden. I can still work because most of the milk brought to the plant comes from the farms owned by the N.S.B. members, and because nearly all of it is used to feed the army around here, the Germans need me at the plant."

Father lights his pipe and sits down.

"I sometimes steal the milk and cheese I take home. We're fortunate to have enough fuel and wood to keep us warm, but it's a different situation in the bombed cities. Fuel and electricity lines were damaged and have not been repaired. People have makeshift stoves. They use oil lamps and candles for light, and even that is hard to come by. If the Germans find out that anyone has been tampering with anything to make their life a little easier, they will be arrested. And that's why we have to stand up and fight! We can't take this lying down. We have to resist, and protect the innocent people. We have to do the best we can to help the people who need to hide from the enemy. We have to fight for our freedom and stand up for our Queen!"

"Now do you understand why I hesitated to tell you?" he asks. "I'm sorry, but I had to keep it from you because I believed you're too young to know of all this horror."

"I'm sorry, too, Papa, for sneaking around behind your back," I tell him. "Would you let me help? I have to do it, if only for Hanna."

"I will talk to Cor Dekker and the others tomorrow and see what I can do. Are you and I okay now?"

"Yes, we're okay, Pa."

Father takes me in his arms and kisses the top of my head. "Let's see what's cooking in the kitchen, shall we?"

CHAPTER 4

Father goes to the Bloch's house that evening and brings Hanna back for our last sleepover before they have to go. He also brings a heavy trunk and, with Hank's help, hides it in the cellar behind a stack of vegetable crates.

Hanna brought some latkes—fried in lard because there's no oil—but with a dollop of Ma's applesauce they're just as tasty.

We avoid talking about the war. We laugh and talk like old times, but we both know it's just a façade. Then Hanna gets quiet and with a sad little voice she says, "You know we're leaving, but I don't know where we're going. I don't understand why we have to go. I'm so worried and scared. Pa said we can only take a few of our things. I left a few boxes in my bedroom. Could you get them later and keep them for me till I get back? I will send word as soon as I can. Oh, Mieneke, I will miss you so much! I'll write, and please, will you promise to write me too?"

But it's too late. Dear God, it's too late!

We hear the squealing tires of a heavy truck brought to an abrupt stop, and the frightening sounds of soldiers' heavy boots. There are noises of glass breaking and loud pounding on a door.

"Raus, raus, schnell, schnell! Outside, fast, hurry, outside right now!"

We run to the window, and get there just in time to see the soldiers roughly push Sam, Minnie and Davie into a covered army truck. Their few belongings, packed in small suitcases, are thrown in after them and the truck's gate tail is slammed shut.

Hanna screams, "Mamma...Papa!"

She turns and runs to the stairs. Pa is already on the top step and catches her in his arms.

"Let me go! I have to go to my Pa and Ma. They took Davie too!"

"Hush, Hanna, hush! Don't let them hear you! Be quiet, please!"

Hanna struggles, but Pa holds on tight. He covers her mouth with one hand to stifle her screams. Hanna keeps on fighting, but finally she gives in. Her knees seem to buckle and, defeated, she slides down on the floor. Papa puts his arms around her and while stroking her back, he rocks her back and forth.

"It's alright my girl. You're safe with us, hush now. Hanna, sweetheart, be still, okay?" She's still shaking, and sobs, "What's going to happen to them? Where will they take my parents and Davie?"

Pa helps her up and I walk over to her.

"It's going to be okay, Hanna. My father knows what to do," I say and, with my arm around her, we follow Father down the stairs.

We're all shaken up. Mamma takes Hanna in her arms and, with her head on Ma's shoulder, she cries. When she's calmed down, Ma says, "Let's have a cup of tea now, and then we'll talk about what we're going to do next."

I make a pot of tea and we all take a seat at the table.

Papa takes Hanna's hand and says, "As your father already told you, you and your family were supposed to leave tonight from here, and go to a safe place. That will still happen. I've promised your parents that, if something was to happen to them, I would look after you—and I'll keep that promise. You are like our own daughter, and we will make sure you're safe. Our guide will be here later to pick you up. However, now that you're leaving by yourself, we have to change our preparations. I had I.D. cards for a family of four traveling together. I can't use those now, but I do have a card for a young boy." He shows us a picture of a blond, fourteen year old Dutch boy. Ma looks at the picture, gets up and says: "Well, we'd better get busy. We have some work to do."

She goes to the bathroom and comes back with a package of hair bleach.

"It's old, but it might still work. Mieneke, can you mix this bleach in a bowl please? We'd better go behind the coal room, just in case."

Ma asks Hanna to sit down on a chair. She kneels in front of her and says, "I'm so sorry Hanna, but we have to cut your hair, and then we have to bleach it to make you look like the boy in the picture. Can we do that, sweetheart?"

"Yes, we have to Vrouw Jansen. I understand what has to be done."

Mamma gets up and takes the scissors from her pocket. She takes one of Hanna's braids, but when she's about to cut, Hanna jerks her head to the side. With her big brown, teary eyes, she looks up at my mother.

"I'm so scared! Where will they take me, Vrouw Jansen? Will I ever see my family again? Where do you think they went? Will we be all right? Oh, what is happening to all of us?"

Ma chokes back her tears. "They will take you to a safe place, and you will stay with decent people there. We will see each other again, and, when this is all over, you'll come home and be together again with your Pa and Ma and Davie too! We had better get busy now, my child—we don't have any time to waste."

Hanna turns around and lets Ma cut her hair. I hand Ma the bleach and she puts the mixture all over Hanna's head. Forty-five minutes later we go to the bathroom, and when the bleach is rinsed out of her hair, Hanna looks totally different! Her hair is short and yellowish-blond.

She rakes her fingers through her short hair.

"That feels so strange," she says with a slightly trembling voice.

Ma has a pair of pants, a corduroy shirt and a pullover, which are too small for Hank, and tells Hanna to put it all on.

"Run upstairs, Mieneke, and get one of Hank's caps."

"You can keep your own coat," Ma says, but when she removes the star from the garment, the outline of the star is clearly noticeable.

"You can have my coat, Hanna," I say.

Now it's done. Hanna looks like the boy in the picture. When I tidy up the room, I pick up one of her braids and put it in my pocket, I don't know why.

We go back to the kitchen and pack a small bag with a bottle of tea, a few cookies and some bread and cheese. In another bag I put some of my underwear, toiletries, a comb, warm socks and an extra sweater.

And now we sit. We try to eat something, but nobody is hungry. We're all edgy and tense. We don't talk much. We anxiously wait. The wait seems to be forever. The clock above the stove is ticking. It sounds louder with each passing minute.

I hold Hanna's hand. "Write to me as soon as you can, please, Hanna."

"I will, every day—and Mieneke, promise me again to write me too."

The long-awaited knock on the door still startles us. My father opens the door and a woman quickly steps inside.

"Martin," she says and nods. "Are they ready?"

Hanna stands up.

"Where are the others? I thought there were four."

"They were taken last night, Silvia; you'll be taking Hanna by herself."

"I'm so sorry, dear," the woman says, and puts her hand on Hanna's arm.

"Are you ready? We have to go right away."

Hanna tries to stay strong, but her hands are shaky. When she can't do up her coat, and starts to sob, I gently remove her hands and button up the coat for her. We're both crying now.

"Be strong, girls," Papa says. "You will see each other again."

Hanna holds onto me so tight, not wanting to let go.

"I love you."

"I love you too!"

Ma hands Hanna the bags. The woman takes her hand and they're gone, swallowed up by the night.

I don't get dressed the following morning. I wander around in my pajamas all day. I'm sad, confused and feel empty without Hanna. I can't eat anything. I sit at the table, go into the porch, come back in, and go to the front room. I turn around and sit down in Papa's chair with an album with pictures of Hanna and me.

When I go outside, I somehow end up in Hanna's backyard, where I sit down in the swing and slowly swing back and forth, thinking about Hanna, until Ma finds me there.

"Come, Mieneke, you shouldn't be here. The Germans might come back," she says. With her jacket draped over my shoulders, she takes me home.

I go upstairs and lay down on my bed, and with my face buried in Hanna's coat, I sob for hours.

My family lets me be, but when I still don't get ready for school the following morning, Ma comes upstairs and sits down on the edge of my bed.

"This is not helping, Mieneke. It's not helping you, and it's certainly not helping Hanna. You have to be strong and get up. Have something to eat and get dressed for school. Peter will be waiting for you."

When I come around the corner by the church, Peter is already there.

"I'm sorry, Mieneke, but I didn't have a chance to talk to you yesterday. I did talk to your father, and I heard what happened to the Blochs. Thank God Hanna got away safe."

Slowly, so the others can catch up, we ride toward the canal.

"Why is this happening, Peter? What did the Blochs ever do to others? What do those bastard Germans want from all of us? What can we do?"

I get so upset, it makes me cry. Peter puts his hand over mine and we stop.

"Hush now." He takes his handkerchief from his pocket and wipes my tears. "There are things we can do to help. When I talked to your father, he agreed to bring you to the meeting tonight. No more crying now, Mieneke. The others are catching up. Let's go, before they wonder what the hell is going on!"

I take his handkerchief and blow my nose. I almost hand it back to him, but I put it in my own pocket.

"Oops, I'd better wash that first!"

"That's my girl!" Peter says and we both laugh.

Peter always makes me feel better.

CHAPTER 5

Dinner is early that evening. The meeting is at six o'clock.

"Martin, are you sure it's a good idea to take Mieneke? I don't like it. We don't all have to stick our neck out! I know I'm being selfish, but she's too young! Are you sure you want to go to the meeting, Mieneke?"

"Yes Mamma, I'm sure. I have to do what I can to help Hanna and others. They need us and I can't turn a blind eye. Please understand Ma, and don't worry. I will be careful and listen to you and Pa."

"We won't have her do anything she can't handle, Anna. We'd better go now. I'll talk to you after the meeting dear."

We're at the Dekker's house a few minutes before six. Peter opens the door to the garden shed, and motions us to come inside. There's a bike tipped over on its seat and handlebar.

"We fix a lot of bikes in here, Mieneke," Peter's Pa says, and winks at me.

I know it's just an excuse for if we get some unexpected "visitors".

There's a pot of coffee on the small pot-belly stove, and Peter pours a cup for each of us.

"I do understand you want to help," Meneer Dekker says. "At first we were a little leery, honestly. You're still young, but then again, you're almost the same age as our Peter. And it might be a good thing to have a young girl like you working with us. You probably won't draw too much attention when it comes to illegal activities."

He continues: "There are important details about our safety, and the safety of the people we help. Secrecy is very important. You can't talk to anybody about what we do. Do not trust anybody! Your Pa will explain all of it later. Now we'd better get started. Martin?" Cor Dekker looks at Pa and nods.

"We have several people hiding in the woods, in houses around town and on the farms." Pa says. "We bring the people in the woods food and supplies as often as we can, and we try to have extra food coupons for the ones hiding elsewhere." Father takes a sip of his coffee.

"We've just got a shipment of food stamps. It came a lot later than we expected. The men in the woods must be running very low on food. We also got a few I.D. cards, which is good. It gets tricky to help people to safe hiding places without these cards. So, this is what needs to be done."

Pa empties his cup and sits down on an empty crate.

"We have to use the food stamps right away. Usually Peer Winters and Peter get the supplies, but Herman Winter had an accident and Peer is needed at the farm. That's why we want you to go with Peter, Mieneke.

"The stamps can only be used in a few stores. We have to shop in the city; there's more food available and not many people know you there.

"We'll give you and Peter enough stamps for two trips—some for tomorrow, and the day after we'll give you the rest. You can't have too many groceries in your bags in case you get stopped and questioned by the Germans, but if you do, you'll tell them you have groceries for Opa and Oma, and for some other people in town."

"Go to two stores tomorrow and get as much as possible. Try to do all the shopping during your lunch break. If you don't get it all done, then try to go again during one of your spare hours. Try to go home with your regular group; if that's not possible, than give Mieneke a five-minute head start, Peter. I don't think it's good to have just the two of you go home with that many groceries.

"When you get back to town, you'll come to the plant. Come around the mill to the back. I'll be waiting for you by the back door. The next day you'll use the rest of the stamps. You know the drill, Peter."

"I have two I.D. cards for you, Peter," Cor Dekker says. "Drop them at the same place as last time, son. There's a card for you too, Mieneke. Your father will give you instructions before you leave for school in the morning. Do you have any questions? No? Okay, in that case, we're done for tonight."

Pa gets up. "We'd better go home now. Say hello to the wife Cor. We should get together soon."

"Yes, we should. Helma would like that. She hasn't been out of the house for a while. The women probably have some catching up to do. Promise me to be careful out there, Martin."

"I always am, Dekker. We'd better go. It's almost eight o'clock and we have a curfew!" Pa says with a wry smile.

I look back over my shoulder to the garden shed. Peter waves before we turn onto the road.

It's already getting dark. There's a soft drizzly rain. The moon is partly hidden behind the clouds and the wet cobblestone glistens in its soft light. It's so quiet and peaceful as I ride home beside Pa. It's hard to believe we're in the middle of a war. We don't talk. The church clock strikes eight as we step into the porch.

Everybody is home and sit at the table, playing a game of cards. Uncle Jan and Aunt Jenny are visiting and plan to stay overnight. Ma puts the kettle on and Hank gathers up the cards and puts them away. Jenny puts the teapot and cups on the table. When we all have a cup in front of us, Father starts to talk.

"As you know now, Mieneke, it was a hard call for us whether or not we should get you involved. First because of your age, but second, as your mother said earlier, we would have one more loved one to worry about. However, we do all agree you'll be able to handle it. You're smart and tough enough to take the pressure, we believe. Everybody here, Cor Dekker, Peter and Paul de Wal—you saw him the other night at the meeting—are part of our group.

"There are others, but you don't need to know who they are until you have to work with them. We're just one team, small fish in a large pond, but we're an important link in the fight against the Nazis. We only take actions on our own, if we absolutely have no other choice. When we receive our orders we carry them out, and pass on information, news and whatever else that needs to be done to the next team."

"We work with a network of only trusted contacts, and everything we tell you is highly confidential, of course. Never talk to anybody about what we do, and be very careful when you talk to each other. Always make sure you can't be overheard. If ever asked, you don't know anything or anybody," Pa says.

He continues: "Your mother and Aunt Jenny look after the people we're hiding downstairs in the plant. Now that the feed department is closed, nobody ever goes down there anymore. It's perfect to hide the ones on the way to a more permanent hiding place. We also distribute the illegal newspaper from there. Uncle Jan and Hank are in charge of that.

That's all for now I believe. If there is anything you need to know you can ask anyone of us. We'll get everything ready before you leave for school in the morning."

I don't sleep much that night. Everything I was told today goes around and around in my head, and I think of Hanna. *Is she okay? Did she make it alright? Where did they take her? Where did the Germans take her family? So much uncertainty! So many questions!*

I hear music and I see Hanna walk toward me.

"Davie is playing the piano for us, Mieneke. Give me your hands and we will dance to his beautiful music!" Hanna, with buttercups and daisy garlands in her beautiful thick hair, is dancing around and around. The skirt of her white Sunday dress swirls around her and, standing on the tip of her toes, she twirls and turns like a ballerina. "Come here, Mieneke, come dance with me. Come Mieneke!"

"Come Mieneke, come on, it's time to get up."

Ma is calling from the bottom of the stairs.

Hanna? That couldn't have been a dream. I didn't sleep! Hanna? I sit up and slowly remove the quilt. Then I remember that today is the day to get the groceries. I'm nervous. I get up and go downstairs and pour myself a cup of tea before I sit down at the table.

"Do you want me to make your lunch?" Ma asks. "Your father should be back any minute now."

My mother fusses over me. I know she's worried.

"Here sweetheart, I boiled an egg for you. You can have it with a slice of bread." An egg! That's a special treat on a school day! It makes my mother feel better to spoil me, I think.

Pa comes home from his daily morning visit with Opa and Oma.

"Here's some coffee from Oma; she can't drink the stamp coffee, she says. It upsets her stomach. Good morning, Mieneke. Did you sleep well?"

"Not that good, Papa, but I'll be okay."

Pa sits down at the table. He seems nervous too.

"Here are the stamps. Put them in your wallet, but zip it up. And here is the I.D. card."

He opens a school textbook. Inside the book, a card is cleverly hidden.

"You'll give the book to your Algebra teacher, Meneer Hendriks. He'll give it back to you at the end of class. If you get caught with this, say you just got the book from the library and don't know anything about the card. Put it in the bag between your others books, okay sweetheart?"

Ma sits down with us and takes my hand.

"Are you sure you want to do this? You can still say no, and that'll be the end of it. We'll understand. We can always find another way."

"Your mother is right. You don't have to do it."

"I'm alright. I want to do it. Now please stop worrying. I'll be fine."

"Okay, my girl, you'd better get ready then. Wear your rain coat—it's pouring outside. I'd better go to work now. I'll see you when you come home. Be careful, okay?"

"I will Pa."

Ma looks worried when, standing in the door, she sees me off.

"I love you," she says. "I love you too, Ma, I'll see you tonight."

It's just Peter waiting by the church. The others are way ahead already.

"Are you ready to fight the Germans?" Peter, almost jokingly, asks.

"As ready as I'll ever be. What's the plan Peter?"

"We'll try to make it to two stores during our lunch hour and get as much as we can. If we don't use all the stamps, then I'll go back at three during my spare hour. Hopefully the line-ups aren't too long. We load you up first, so you can go home with the others. If I'm back late, I'll go home with Tom. He has a late class and is done at four fifteen. I'll meet you at the front door at noon, okay? Good plan?"

"Yes, good plan. We'd better hurry up and catch up with the others."

A strong, nasty wind blows across the canal, pelting the cold rain in our face. It makes biking hard and tiring. Peter pushes me in my back to give me a little boost. I really like Peter. He's always so helpful and sweet.

We finally make it to school, and walk in just before the front doors close.

I'm tense now, and it's hard to pay attention during my first class. At eleven o'clock, when on my way to Algebra class, I see Peter. He winks and gives me a thumb up. It relaxes me somewhat, and I quickly enter the classroom before the other students come in.

Meneer Hendriks is already in the room cleaning the blackboard.

"Good morning Meneer Hendriks." He nods when I put the book on his desk. "Good morning Mieneke."

I take a deep breath and sit down at my desk. That's one thing done!

The wind is howling around the building and the rain beats against the windows. Most students keep their heavy sweaters on. It's cold in the room.

Class seems to go on forever and I get more fidgety with each passing minute. Finally the teacher gives us our homework. "Study lessons 27, 28 and 29. Exams are on Thursday." And the lunch bell rings.

I take my time to put my stuff away, and linger long enough for the other students to leave the room. When Meneer Hendriks gives me a short nod, I swipe the book off his desk and quickly slip it into my bag.

"Thank you, Meneer Hendriks."

"Thank you too Mieneke."

I walk as fast as I can through the long hall to meet up with Peter.

"Hi kid, are you ready?" When I nod, he says, "Okay, follow the leader."

It's still raining, and we stop under a store's awning to talk.

"We go to the store the furthest away first, the one around the corner from the theater. Then we go to the one just a block away from our school."

There are only a few people ahead of us when we enter the store. We get enough groceries to fill my side-bags. By the time we get to the other store, the rain has lightened up. We're not so lucky here. There's a long line of people waiting and the shelves are almost empty. We get whatever we can.

"There is another shipment on Thursday," the woman behind the counter says.

"I know of another store," Peter says. "I'll go there at three. You did good Mieneke."

We put our bikes away and rush into the school. So far, so good! Now we only have to make it home. I feel hungry now. We forgot to eat our lunch! I collect myself and make an effort to listen to the teacher.

Peter isn't there when I get to the bike racks, at the end of our school day.

"Have you seen Peter, Margie?"

"He was in science class earlier, and I see that his bike is still here. Peer is waiting by the gate, and I don't think Peter is with him. Are you okay?"

"Yeah, I'm fine," I say, but I'm nervous now. I don't want to go home without Peter. Margie seems to sense that something is bugging me.

"We can wait for a few minutes," she says.

Just as we get our bikes out of the rack and are ready to leave, Peter comes running across the schoolyard. "Wait up, guys!" He quickly checks the bags and we're off.

It is still windy, but the rain has stopped, and with the strong wind now pushing us in our back it's like sailing all the way home.

There's some commotion on the big intersection by the first bridge. When we come closer we see four German soldiers stop all traffic to let a column of army vehicles through.

We're waiting only a few meters away from two soldiers who smoke a cigarette and watch the trucks go by. One of the soldiers keeps looking in our direction.

I can feel Peter looking sideways at me.

"Relax" he says under his breath.

My legs feel like rubber when the soldiers finally wave us through.

"Good job, girl," Peter says and hands me half of his sandwich.

"Thanks Peter. I was hungry earlier, but I can't eat a bite now!"

"Sure you can. It'll make you feel better; eat up!"

Pa is waiting by the back door.

"Thank goodness, you're here! Quickly, come in, and bring your bikes inside, too. You had no problems? Everything went okay?"

"Yes, everything went smooth Meneer Jansen, and Mieneke did a great job."

Peter and Pa empty the bags and stow everything in a space underneath the stairs.

"I'd better go now. I'll see you tomorrow?"

"Go straight home, Peter. Your Pa asked about you earlier."

"I will. See you tomorrow."

"Wait for me, Mieneke. I'll lock up and then we can go, too." Pa says.

They're all happy to see me.

"I was worried about you all day!" Ma says.

"Good job Sis!"

Hank gives me a wet, sloppy kiss.

"Yuck! Get away from me!"

I poke his ribs. I know he's ticklish and chase him around the table.

"Stop, Mieneke—I'm sorry! Please stop!"

"You started it, and now I'm going to get you!"

"Both of you stop right now! Dinner is ready!"

It's the same routine the next day. We have a few stamps left when our lunch hour is over, but Peter will go to the store near our school at three.

"The woman said they will have a shipment on Thursday. That's today, right?"

"Yes, that's today."

"Okay—I'll see you at four."

When we empty the bags at the plant, I notice that the storage room is empty.

"What happened to the groceries we brought yesterday Pa?"

"Oh, they're gone already. It doesn't make sense to have them here. They're needed, Mieneke."

I wonder if that's what Uncle Jan and Pa were doing last night.

It does get easier every time we do a grocery run, but we're always careful. Sometimes we can't go, like the time Meneer Hendriks told me it was better to wait another day.

"The Germans are on the prowl. They stop everybody to check for I.D. We'd better not take any chances."

CHAPTER 6

January, 1944 - November, 1944

After I've done all my chores one Saturday afternoon, Ma asks me to take a pint of milk to Opa and Oma's.

I stop at Margie's to see if she wants to tag along. Margie and I spend a lot of time together. I like her and she's not nearly as shy as I always thought she was. She's smart and funny, and she makes me laugh.

We talk about school, about boys, the war, and about our plans for when we've finished school.

"I want to be a landscape designer, like my father was. I want to create beautiful gardens and city parks. We still have lots of my Pa's books and I've gone through most of them. I find it very interesting, and I would love to study that! That is, if this bloody war ever ends, and if we'll ever finish school! I couldn't believe it when the principal told us that we can only attend classes three days a week now. Quite a few teachers are gone, have you noticed? The Nazis took my English teacher during class! They just busted through the doors! One minute he was standing there, writing our assignment on the blackboard, and the next minute he was gone! I notice that others have been taken too, and nobody has seen them ever since!" Margie says.

"Another reason why our school hours have been cut is because there's not enough fuel to keep the building warm; haven't you noticed how cold it is some days? I just hope that we're not told to stay home for the whole winter!"

We move over to the side when we hear the ring of a bicycle bell, but the bikers stop.

"Good afternoon, Fraulein."

A tall German soldier steps of his bike. He has a scar across his left cheek and when he smiles, the left corner of his mouth goes up, and his eye closes, as if he's winking at us. With him is a woman. She wears high heels and a beautiful coat with a fur collar, unlike Margie's and my coat, which have been lengthened and let out so many times. The heavy socks in our wooden shoes are less flattering than her fancy high heels for sure!

"Hi Margie, hi Mieneke," the woman says, and then we recognize her. It's Coba Mos! She was a year ahead of us in school, and started working at the hotel, the one now occupied by the Germans, right after she finished grade six. She doesn't look anything like the mousy girl we remember. She looks like a Hollywood movie star!

Her hair is bleached out to a high blond and curled, her eyebrows are shaved and penciled in with a fine line, and her lips are as red as Hanna's raspberry candies.

"Wow, Coba! You look so different! We didn't recognize you! How come we never see you around? Don't you play ball anymore?"

"No I don't, basketball is for kids. I have more important things to do now. By the way, this is Werner Zimmerman, my boyfriend. Werner organized a dance. It is tonight in the old gym. We could use a few more girls—would you like to join us?"

"Gee, Coba, I don't know if my parents would let me, and with curfew and all…"
"Curfew is no problem if you have German friends, right Werner?" Coba says.

She looks up to her boyfriend with an admiring smile.

"Werner can pick you up in his car. You should come. It'll be fun. And how about you—will you come, Margie?"

"I wouldn't get permission to go, no hope in hell. Besides, I don't have anything to wear to a dance!"

"Oh, let's go already, Werner," says Coba, and she pulls Scarcheek along by his arm.

"Who wants them there anyways? They're just little wimps!"

"Ah, we're not good enough for you?" he says in his German accent.

"Come Werner, let's go!"

"You're nothing but little bitches!" Coba yells as they ride away.

"Holy cow, what was that all about?" I say. "I didn't even see it was Coba. She looks like a…like a…"

"A Nazi whore," Margie says.

"Margie, how do you know what a Nazi whore looks like?"

"Just like Coba Mos!" And we both start to laugh.

We're still laughing when we walk into Oma's kitchen.

"What's so funny?" Oma asks.

We tell her about our little encounter with Coba and her German boyfriend.

"What are the parents thinking, letting a young girl hang around riffraff like that? Nothing to laugh about, girls! It's a bloody shame!" Oma shakes her head.

"Where's Opa?"

"He's in the garden. Why don't you call him in, and I'll put the kettle on. It's almost teatime."

Opa waves when he sees us come through the garden gate.

"Well, look who's here! You girls finally found some time to spent with this old man?"

"Opa really! You're not that old. What are you doing?"

"Just a bit of gardening to keep me busy, girls."

He's dug a deep hole and now lowers a heavy bag into it.

"Isn't it too cold for gardening? And what's in that bag, Opa?"

"The two of you are too smart for your own good! I have some copper pots and pans, some kitchen utensils and other copper and metal things in this bag. I heard the German confiscate all this stuff to make bullets with. They even steal the church bells, I was told. This stuff might not be worth anything, but I, as sure as hell, will not hand it over to the Nazis—but no tattling young ladies!"

He throws a shovel full of dirt in the hole.

"Do you need a hand, Opa? Oma wants you to come in for tea."

"The two of you go ahead. It won't take long to cover this bag. We'd better not let the old girl wait!"

After we have our tea and are ready to go home, Oma puts a loaf of fresh bread in a bag for me to take home. She doesn't bake bread as often as she used to, since flour is rationed, but she still likes to share.

"And here is one for your Ma, too, Margie—and thank you both for bringing the milk. Now go straight home. No dillydallying!"

"Would you like to come to my house and have supper with us, Margie?"

"I would love to, but I'd better go home. Ma isn't feeling very well, and I don't know what Tom is doing tonight. Ma gets so worried every time he's out after curfew. I can come over tomorrow afternoon if you like. Ma takes a nap at around one o'clock every day."

"Yes, let's get together tomorrow, that'll be great!"

We're all home Saturday evening. We play cards and Uncle Jan recalls some funny anecdotes from the time he and Pa were little boys.

"This one evening after supper, we snuck out of the house to steal apples in a farmer's yard and..."

"Oh, here we go!" Pa says.

Uncle Jan snickers. "Anyway, your father climbed up high in the apple tree. I stood underneath catching the apples. All of a sudden, the farmer comes running out of the house holding a gun! 'What are you kids doing here? Stealing my apples?' he said!"

Uncle Jan is laughing, and continues. "I ran and jumped over this real high hedge. I never even knew I could jump that high! Fear, I guess!"

"Yes, you always were a little coward, for sure!" Pa says.

"Never mind, brother!" Uncle Jan goes on. "Your Pa is still up in the tree. The farmer points his pellet gun and shoots up through the branches. He wasn't seriously trying to hit your Pa, but just wanted to scare us a bit. However, one of the pellets hits your father's behind. He comes sliding down the branches, bawling his eyes out! 'You'd better get out of here and go home straight away or I have to tell your parents what you've been up to!' the farmer yells at him."

"Of course we had to tell Oma—she had to get the pellet out! It was a good thing Opa wasn't home or your Pa's butt would've hurt a lot more!"

"Oh, for Pete's sake Jan! Do you all see how much trouble he used to get me into? It wasn't even worth it! The apples weren't ripe yet and were still green and hard, just sour little things—yuck!"

We all have a good laugh.

"I'll bet your parents and the farmer had a good laugh too!" Aunt Jenny says.

Margie comes over on Sunday after lunch. We take a stack of photo albums, a pot of tea and some cookies upstairs and, snuggled underneath my quilt, we go through all the pictures.

"It's no wonder Coba called us little wimps! Look at you here! That big bow in your hair is bigger than your whole head!"

"Oh, really? And who's that girl in this picture? The one who's missing her two front teeth? Isn't that you?"

We both laugh when we see a picture of Tom, Peter and Peer all dressed up in their Easter clothes. New shorts, knee-high socks and brand new shirts. Their hair is perfectly parted and styled with their father's hair cream.

"Oh, here's a picture of Hanna with her new bike. Isn't she cute? I remember when she got that bike for her birthday."

"Have you heard anything, Mieneke? Do you know where she is? And do you know where her family is?"

"No, we don't know where they took her parents and Davie. Pa told me Hanna got away and is safe, but hasn't told me where she is—maybe he doesn't know. I wanted to go back into their house, to get Hanna's boxes, but father forbid me. He went in one night, but everything is gone he said. He thinks the Germans want to use the house for storage. Nobody has moved in. Pa told me the Germans came back after the arrest, and ransacked the house. They took whatever they wanted I guess, and made a pile in the courtyard with the rest of the stuff, which they burned. There's nothing left worth saving, Pa said."

"We should go in and check it out."

"We would be in so much trouble Margie if we were caught. Besides, there's a sign on the door that says, 'Eingang Verboten!' We're not allowed to go inside."

"Oh please, since when do you abide by the rules? Come on, let's go! I know you want to! It's shouldn't be too hard to get in; there are probably enough broken windows."

"Okay, let's go, let's do it!"

"We'll go for a little walk Ma, we won't go far."

"I'm having tea at Oma's. See you when I get home!"

We go through the back to the Bloch's house. There is one broken window that is not boarded up, and a weather-beaten curtain hangs out of it. It smells musty and smoky when we move it aside to crawl inside. The pretty window screens are broken and the lace is blackened from smoke.

It's freezing inside. The house is in shambles.

The kitchen table is tipped over and chairs are broken in pieces. Odds and ends left behind are either broken, molded or water damaged.

The dining room is empty. The cabinet and all the crystal, dishes and silver have disappeared. The Menorah, polished so faithfully every week, is gone too.

I sift through the rubble and pick up two pieces of a cup. When I put them together and they fit, I can read the inscription and I tear up.

"Remember the Sabbath and keep it Holy."

I put the broken pieces in my pocket.

We walk through Sam's shop. The wooden cabinets are gone and so are the rolls of material and textiles. There are no sewing machines anymore and the boxes with needles, trims and buttons are strewn all over the floor.

I pick up Sam's pencil stub and put it in my pocket too.

Upstairs in the master bedroom, we find Minnie and Sam's mattress destroyed; red paint is deliberately poured all over it. The paint can is still there.

"Judische Swine, Jewish Pigs," is painted on the wall above the bed. The red paint ran down to the floor and dried on the wall like long streams of blood.

Margie finds a flattened shoebox box, barely noticeable underneath the mattress. In it are pictures, school scribblers and report cards from Davie and Hanna.

"Let's take this box and get the hell out of here!"

"One more room, please Margie. I want to see Hanna's room."

There's nothing left in her room. Her boxes are gone and scribblers and pictures are torn up and thrown in a corner. I find Hanna's little silver jewelry box between the papers. I'm crying now.

When we go down the stairs, I see something shiny in the corner of my eye, and bent over to have a closer look. It's Hanna's ladybug ring! I try to pull it out from between the wooden floor planks, but can't get a grip on it. Margie finds a nail and manages, after some wiggling, to wedge it underneath the silver band and she jerks it out. The ring was flattened and scratched when stomped on by a heavy boot, but the Ladybug is still intact. Tears are running down my face.

"Oh Hanna—poor Hanna! Let's get out of here Margie, this is too horrible!"

I follow Margie down the stairs, when suddenly she stops and turns around.

"Quick, back upstairs," she whispers. "Somebody is coming!"

I can hear it now too. Somebody is opening the back door! We go back upstairs, as fast and quietly as we can, and I step into Hanna's closet to hide.

"No, not there, that's the first place they look! Help me, come here, hurry up and help me with the mattress."

We lean the mattress against the wall, and quickly crawl into the space between it and the wall.

We can hear voices downstairs. Somebody is laughing, and there's a lot of noise. The loud banging of a hammer bounces off the walls and the hollow sounds echo through the empty house. We're so scared!

The hammering stops, and a few seconds later we hear a door slam shut. It's quiet. We stay behind the mattress, with our arms around each other, for a few more minutes, and when we think they're gone, we carefully go down the stairs. There's a stack of boxes in the kitchen now, and bicycles are stored in the porch.

"My God, that was close! Let's get out of here!" Margie whispers.

We turn to the broken window, but its shut! Two planks are nailed across, and we're trapped! We try all the windows and doors, but can't find one that opens. We go back upstairs and finally manage to pry Davie's bedroom window open. Looking down, we see that we have to climb through the window onto the porch roof, and then slide down the rain-pipe onto the ground.

"I'll go first, hold my hand, so I won't slide down too fast," Margie says. She's already hanging out of the window.

Oh, please, don't let anybody see us! Margie is on the porch roof. I look down and hand her the box with pictures.

"Come on, legs first, and I'll grab you to slow you down—hurry, Mieneke!"

We have to slide down the pipe next. Margie goes first. She is on the ground already, but just before I reach her, the lining of my coat catches on something and I can hear it rip. Darn! We quickly pull it free, and run home through the courtyard and the back gardens. Thank God nobody saw us!

We're cold and in a morbid mood when we come home.

"Phew! That was a close call!! I'm still shaking. Can you fix your coat?"

"Yes, I'll be okay, it's just the liner."

"That was bad—*very* bad—but we made it, and at least we got that box with the pictures."

"Yes! And Hanna's ring! I hope we have enough time to clean the Bloch's house before they come home. It looks so terrible!"

"We will all come and help when that time comes, don't worry."

"You're a good friend, Margie."

"And so are you Mieneke. Come here and give me a hug!"

We can hear Ma downstairs.

"Are you having supper with us, Margie?" she asks, when we come down the stairs.

"Thank you, Vrouw Jansen, but Ma is home alone and I'd better go."

"How is your Ma these days?"

"Oh, she's not too bad. It has been quite a few years now since Papa passed away, and things have gotten a little easier, but she's never really been the same; we manage, though."

"Here is a piece of cheese to take home to your Ma. Tell her I will come for a visit soon."

"She'll like that, Vrouw Jansen, thank you. I'll see you tomorrow, Mieneke."

CHAPTER 7

We have a big ham for Christmas this year. Pa and Cor Dekker butchered a pig, illegally of course, and now there's ham, pork chops, bacon and a dozen sausages hang to dry underneath the cellar's staircase.

"We'll have a full house tonight," Ma says. "With Opa and Oma and Hank's guest, there are nine of us!"

"Who's Hank's guest?"

"Anneke Oostra, his new girlfriend, is coming for Christmas dinner. He asked me this morning if it was okay. So it's must be serious! 'The more the merrier,' I said."

"Is that's why we'll have our Christmas dinner tonight?"

"Yes. Anneke has a big family. There are seven girls and three boys. They will have dinner together tomorrow. Opa and Opa come here again on Christmas day for left overs."

"Huh, I didn't even know they're dating. I like Anneke. Remember we used to play ball together? Is she still working at the post office?"

"Yes, she is. I always liked her too. Mieneke, please, peel the potatoes. Here's the pan. Make sure you peel enough!"

Hank and Anneke walk in an hour later.

"Hey Anneke, that's a surprise! I didn't know you're dating my ugly brother! He's so sneaky!"

"You don't have to know everything right away, nosy Nelly!" Hank says.

"Well! You could have told your only sister, Carrot top!" I say, calling him by his old nickname. "How long have you been dating?"

"Just a few months now, but I've had my eyes on her a lot longer!"

"Oh please, you never even noticed me—besides, we've been dating for almost six months," Anneke laughs.

"You must be done school now, Mieneke?"

"Yes, but they closed the school for the winter to save fuel, I guess. We have a few more exams to write, but we were promised that we can finish this coming spring."

Oma and Opa bring dessert: Raisins and brandy with cream.

"I've kept this hidden a long time, but you can't keep things forever—besides, it's Christmas," Oma says.

"It's like a good old-fashioned Christmas," Aunty Jenny says, and she ladles the raisins in Ma's fancy dessert bowls.

Before we put the food away and do the dishes, Pa takes a few bowls with left-overs and says, "I'll be back in a flash, Anna."

When Ma sees the puzzled look on my face, she tells me that a mother and her little girl are staying downstairs at the plant. They came the night before last, and Oma and Anneke will take them to a hiding place near the city on Christmas day.

"We'd planned to wait another day, but the Germans celebrate Christmas too. It should be quiet on the road tomorrow. Christmas day is as good a day as any, probably safer." Oma says.

"I'll go with Anneke, Oma. It's too cold for you to bike all the way to the city. I'll go, if you don't mind."

"That would be nice, Mieneke, but wait till your father is home; let's see what he has to say."

Father agrees. "Why didn't I think of that myself? Okay girls, sit down please. I've already told the woman this. I have two I.D. cards, but unfortunately, I don't have two with the same last name. If questioned, the story you tell is that her daughter is her little niece. I hope the child doesn't say anything! In any case, you'll know how to handle it, Anneke. Bring some warm clothes—their coats are thin and it's cold outside!"

"Pa, where are we taking them?"

"You'll be taking them to the Hendriks. Albert Hendriks—your teacher—and his mother will take them in. They live just on the outskirts of the city. It's not too far, maybe fifteen, twenty minutes at the most, but you know where they live. You'll pick them up in the morning from the plant. You can only take two bikes. I wish we had another bike, but then again, you would have to leave it behind. The woman is young, in her early thirties I would say. She shouldn't have a problem with taking turns biking."

Opa and Oma leave at seven thirty. "Be careful tomorrow, girls." Opa says.

Ma puts a blanket and a pillow on the sofa for Anneke. We play cards and finish the rest of the raisins before we all go to bed.

We bundle up, put some warm clothes in our bags, and Ma hands us a few sandwiches for the mother and her girl.

"Please, repeat the instructions to me," Anneke asks the mother, after we meet her at the plant. She remembers what my Pa told her and tells us not to worry about her daughter. "She might not understand why, but she knows not to talk."

"We brought you a sandwich; you can eat it on the way—is that okay?"

"Yes, that's very nice. Thank you for doing this. I know how dangerous it is, so thank you. Without people like you, we wouldn't have made it this far."

"Don't worry. We're all in this together. We want you and your little girl to be safe. You can sit behind me, it's not that far. Maybe we change seats later and you can bike the rest of the way. Now, you'd better dress warm, and then we'll go."

"Hi," I say to the little girl. She's so cute and shy. When she looks at me, with her big brown eyes, she reminds me of Hanna.

"I'm Mieneke. Let me help you to get on the back of my bike. Put one leg on this side and in the bag and the other one in this bag. There you go! Are you comfy? Are you hungry? Here's your sandwich, sweetheart. Ready? Let's go."

There's nobody on the road when we leave the plant. We take the back road to the city. It's a little longer, but safer. I'm glad we took this road, because it's sheltered by large trees and not nearly as cold as riding along the canal.

We stop to let an army truck go through when we have to cross the road to get on the bike path. We're a little tense, but the vehicle keeps going.

We meet two couples on the way to town, and we greet them cheerfully, "Merry Christmas!"

When we turn into the long driveway toward the farm house, I see Meneer Hendriks already waiting in the front door.

"Merry Christmas, Mieneke, it's good to see you! And Merry Christmas to you too, Anneke! Please, come in. Welcome to our home," he says to the woman.

"The coffee is ready, and for you, little lady, I have hot chocolate—and how about a cookie? Ma, our guests are here!"

"Ah, there you are! We were waiting for you! Please come in! Come in and make yourself at home. I'm Oma Hendriks, and this is my son, Albert."

The old woman fusses over the little girl. She takes her coat and shows her around the house.

"There's a box with toys in the corner over there; we can take them upstairs and I'll show you your room. Albert, please pour the coffee and we'll be back in a minute!"

"Let me put your coat away. Sit down! You must be tired. I'll show you around the house later, but first, relax and make yourself at home. Sit down, Anneke—you too, Mieneke."

"Would you like cream in your coffee, ladies?" he asks, while pouring the coffee.

"Are we staying here? We're here? Oh thank you, thank you so much!"

The young woman puts her face in her hands and starts to cry.

"I'm sorry, but it was so hard. I don't mean to cry. My name is Betty Weiser, and my daughter's name is Sahra. It has been a while since I told anybody my real name," she says, and holds out her hand.

"How long were you and Sahra on the road, Betty?" Meneer Hendriks asks.

"We left right away after I found out my husband and my two sons were taken. I was warned not to go home. The Germans were waiting for us. One of my neighbors met me on the way home and took me to her brother. I don't know where they took my husband and my boys. I'm so worried, and Sahra, poor little soul, doesn't understand why we had to go without her Papa and brothers. We didn't have I.D. cards, and could only travel by night. My neighbors' brother arranged for us to meet with people who could help us. They live in Delft, about twenty-five kilometers away from where we live, and he took us there. It's been two weeks since we left Delft. Two long, scary weeks," she sighs.

"Well, you can relax now Betty. You'll stay here with us. Look, who's that girl coming down the stairs?" Meneer Hendriks says when Sahra comes in.

"Did you come to get your hot chocolate, and do you like your room, Sahra?"

"Yes," she says, and looks at him with a smile. A little shy, but a happy smile.

"And Mamma, we have a room together, so we won't be lonely, Oma Hendriks says, and we can see the new puppies after, and…"

"Slow down, sweetheart, slow down," her mother laughs. "Drink your chocolate now, okay?"

We leave soon after we finished our coffee, and I'm grateful Betty and Sahra found such a happy home.

"I didn't know you are part of the team, Anneke," I say to her on the way home.

"That's how Hank and I got together. Sometimes I help with the newspaper or with the supplies; wherever I'm needed, that's where I go," Anneke laughs.

"Now you know."

"I sure hope Hanna found people as nice as the Hendriks to stay with. It must be so hard, not knowing where you're going or if you'll ever make it there!"

"Hanna did find a good place Mieneke. Hank told me how close you and Hanna were. You'll see her again. Always remember to keep your chin up! Hank said she's safe."

We hear a vehicle come up from behind. The car slows down to our speed and proceeds to drive beside us. "Scarcheek" Werner Zimmerman leans out of the passenger's window.

"Ah, we meet again. Hello Mieneke, Merry Christmas Fraulein. We're looking for some fun ladies to join us tonight for dinner. There will be a fantastic Christmas spread and a big celebration after. How about it, what do you think? Would you and your friend like to come for a nice meal and some drinks?"

"No, we'll have dinner with our family tonight, thank you."

"We're still not good enough for you? Is that right?"

"I'd rather starve than eat with your kind," I mumble under my breath.

"I heard that. You're one stupid girl. You'd better watch your big mouth. That could very well happen. You might never eat again and starve to death. You'll be sorry one day! Go," he yells at the driver, who hits the gas pedal. With squealing tires, they speed away, leaving a spray of pebbles in their wake.

"Mieneke, you have to watch what you say to those guys! That wasn't very smart! Jeez, that was dangerous! Don't provoke them! You're playing right into their hands! Don't you ever do that again!"

"I'm sorry, but he made me so mad! Every time I see him he gets under my skin—he's so creepy!"

"Don't get mad—get even! I get mad and frustrated too—we *all* do—but you have to bite your tongue and keep your mouth shut! Let's go home."

I feel so stupid and immature now. *I have to control my temper! What's wrong with me?* I think.

"I'm sorry, you're right, I shouldn't have said that. I feel real stupid."

"It's okay. You've learned your lesson. We'll keep it between us. It's okay, don't worry about it anymore."

"Thank you, it'll never happen again. I promise."

"Good. Let's get going."

Before I go to bed, I take Hanna's ladybug ring out of the box.

"I almost blew it today, Hanna. I have to control my temper! I'm keeping your ring on me from now on and every time, when I'm tempted to open my big mouth, I'll touch it and count to ten! Happy Hanukah; and goodnight Hanna."

I put the ring on a thin silver chain and clasp it around my neck.

CHAPTER 8

I think I'm in love. Every time I see Peter and look into his steel-grey eyes, I get butterflies in my stomach. Peter always makes me feel safe and secure when I'm near him. He so smart and so handsome! He's long-legged, broad-shouldered, and has a flawless, square-jawed face. I would love to run my hands through his tousled, thick sandy blond hair; I wonder what it would feel like to rest my head on those strong shoulders and have his arms around me.

Peter doesn't know this, of course, and I would never reveal my feelings for him. Why would he be interested in me? I don't see myself as attractive. Not at all like some girls from our school. They're so flirty and always seem to know exactly what to say to the boys.

Maybe I should have my hair cut in a newer style. Ma's friend Greet is a hair-dresser, she could do it for me, maybe. I'll ask Ma tonight.

Would Peter notice me then, when I look all modern? Maybe he doesn't like it at all and he'll laugh at me. He likes to tease me, just like Hank always does. He probably sees me like a little sister.

Why is there a rule that girls are not supposed to ask boys out? Ah, maybe just as well—I would be too shy anyways. What if he said no? That would be too embarrassing!

It would be so nice to talk to Hanna right now.

Hank set up the shuffleboard in the loft and invited all our friends for a game. It's Sunday afternoon and we're upstairs. The boys get more competitive with each game. Tom is ahead in points, every time!

"Now that we know who the shuffle champion is, we'd better quit for today. I'll give you a chance for a rematch next week at our house. You'll have a whole week to practice, so no sorry excuses!"

"I'll take you on for a rematch right now, Tom!"

"Please, no, Hank," Anneke groans. "That's enough for today; let's go for a walk, it's beautiful outside!"

"We'd better go home," Tom says. "Ma is expecting us for supper and we don't like to leave her at home by herself for too long. It's Sunday and we should spend some time with her."

It's only March, but already it feels like spring. Crocuses poke their little heads up through the still-patchy grass, and new buds produce a hazy light green aura around the tree branches.

We drop off Margie, Tom and his girlfriend Ina at their home, and continue our walk.

When we come around the church to cross the square, we notice a few German soldiers on the terrace in front of the hotel, enjoying a beer in the afternoon sun.

"It must be nice to be able to live a life of luxury," Hank says. "Let's go the other way, through the alley by the library."

We skip across the schoolyard to the soccer field, where the junior soccer team plays a neighboring town. We sit down on a bench, away from other spectators, and watch the game. It's a close match.

"Does anybody know when school starts again? I wouldn't mind writing those last exams," I ask.

"Yes—my mother ran into one of the teachers on Friday, and he told her we can come back at the end of April. We should know after a week or so if we passed." Peer says.

"Will you be able to go, Peer? How's your father? Is he better now, or do you still have to help on the farm?" I ask.

"He's still not a hundred percent, but I can take a few days here and there to go to classes and to write the exams. Are *you* going, Peter?"

"Absolutely, I'll be there for sure! Man, it would be so nice to be finally done with school!"

A few girls walk by. They went to elementary school with us, but now attend a domestic school in a different town.

"Hi," they say as they pass us. "Hi, Peter," adds Lonny Batten, a cute little brunette. She giggles when she looks back over her shoulder.

"Oh, hi Lonny," Peter says, and I see his face turn red.

It makes me feel uncomfortable.

Peter is late on our first day back to school. When he finally appears around the corner, he's riding his mother's bike.

"Can you believe it? The first school day and those damned Germans take my bike! I told them I need it to go to school, but no! They don't care. Thieves! I had to run back home to get Ma's bike. Pa will try to get it back, but we might as well forget it! Sorry guys, let's go. I've made you all late!"

"Well, there's nothing you can do about it now, Peter; besides you look kind of cute on your mother's bike!"

"Yeah, yeah, I'll get you back for that later, Margie!"

Peter has a girlfriend and it upsets me. Am I jealous? I suppose I am. I have a hard time even talking to him now. Things between us have changed. Peter seems to be occupied and there's not a lot of conversation going on between us on the food runs or the way to school. I ride beside Margie most days.

Sometimes I see Peter and Lonny together on a walk through town, or I pass them on the path to the forest. I'm so unhappy, and feel so lonely. I wish I could talk to Hanna; what would she do? There are days I don't even want to leave the house. Ma must've noticed that there's something's wrong with me, and she's trying to cheer me up, but it irritates me and that makes me feel even worse.

One Saturday afternoon, Greet the hairdresser comes over to our house to do mother's hair.

"Would you like your hair done too, Mieneke? I don't have other appointments this afternoon. There is a new hairstyle that's very popular; it would look really good on you, and your hair is perfect for it," Greet says.

"No, I'm fine. I have a lot of homework this weekend and I'd better go upstairs and study."

"Oh, come on now, Mieneke, a change will do you some good, and you haven't had a new do for so long. Greet is here now, we might as well take advantage of that, don't you think?"

"I don't know; I like my hair the way it is; it isn't that bad, is it?"

"Why don't you have a seat, it'll be fun! Here, have a look at this picture—that's the style I was talking about. It's called a bob. It's so cute, and it would absolutely look great on you!"

"Okay, if you think so," I say, and reluctantly I sit down.

Greet does her magic, and the new hairstyle she creates does suit me. I look in the mirror and see a young woman instead of a teenager. It feels good, and I'm glad they talked me into it.

That same afternoon, Ma and I go through my wardrobe and sort out my clothes. We take out the sewing machine and alter some, and change the look of a few of my outdated outfits.

I feel confident and renewed—even a little sexy, believe it or not!

"Eat your heart, out Peter Dekker!" I say, when I take one more glance in the mirror, before I leave for school.

"Wow, you look good, girl! I love your new haircut!" Margie says. I see Peter glance at me, and a little later he pulls up beside me.

"I like your hair too, Mieneke; you look very nice."

I turn toward him and see he's blushing.

"Thank you Peter," I say, and I feel a flutter in my stomach.

In another few weeks we're done with school. I haven't heard a word from Hanna and now I wonder if I ever will. As time goes by, I miss her more and more. There are so many things I like to talk to her about, and I think about her every day.

I haven't seen Peter and Lonny together for quite a while, and Peter seems to be around his friends, including me, a lot more lately. I wonder if he and Lonny broke up, but Peter doesn't say anything, at least not to me.

Finally curiosity gets the best of me, and when we're a little distance away from the others I ask, "I haven't seen you and Lonny together lately; is everything alright between the two of you?"

"Yea, its fine I suppose. I see her around school, but we don't do things together anymore, and that's okay," he answers. We leave it at that, but I'm relieved.

Most days Peter bikes beside me again.

"Can you slow down a little, Mieneke?" Peter says, one day on the way home from school.

"I uh…I want to ask you something. Umm…I really like spending time with you and…uh…would you like to go for a walk on Sunday afternoon? We could bring some food maybe and have a picnic."

"Yes, I would like that Peter, it sounds like fun…yes…I'll bring a few sandwiches if you like. What time?"

"I'll pick you up at…say…twelve thirty?"

"I'll be ready. See you on Sunday, Peter," I say before I turn into my street.

"Ma, is it okay if I make some sandwiches to take along this afternoon?" I ask Ma, before Peter's suppose to pick me up.

"Sure Mieneke, there's some leftover ham you can have; where are you going?"
"Peter and I are going for a walk later. I thought it would be nice to bring something to eat."

"Yes, that is nice. I like Peter. Is anybody else going?"

"No, just Peter and me Ma…I'll go upstairs now and get dressed."

I'm so nervous! What should I wear, my Sunday dress maybe? No, that might be too much. Maybe the skirt that Aunty Jenny just lengthened for me? After I have taken almost all my clothes out of my closet, I decide to wear my school skirt and the pretty pink sweater Oma knitted for me.

Peter picks me up at exactly twelve thirty. He takes the small basket from me.

"Let me carry that. Where would you like to go?"

"Let's walk over to the look-out. It's a nice walk to the tower, and not too far."

I'm so nervous, but Peter seems so sure of himself.

We walk past the big old owl tree.

"I don't know why people call this the 'Owl tree'—do you?"

"Maybe once upon a time there were owls in this tree."

We look at each other and laugh.

"I'm sorry Peter, but I'm nervous. This is like a date, and I've never been asked on a date before."

"Honestly, I'm nervous too. I wanted to ask you for a while, but I could never work up enough courage. You're so pretty, and I was sure you wouldn't go with me. I like spending time with you. I like you a lot and…uh…uh, well what the heck, will you go…will you be my girlfriend?"

"What about you and Lonny? Is that all done and over with?"

"Yes it is—besides, I was thinking about you all the time when I was dating her and that's the main reason why she and I broke up." Peter is blushing. Oh my God! I want to kiss him right here, right now!

"Oh Peter! I like spending time with you too, and I'm so glad you asked me. I've been thinking of you too!" Jeez! I probably say all the wrong things; I seem too eager! I'm so stupid!

Peter puts the basket down, takes my face between his hands and kisses me, ever so softly, on my lips. An unfamiliar heat curls up my spine and through my whole body. I put my arms around his neck and kiss him back. Oh God, it feels so good!!

We climb to the top of the look-out. We can see for miles from here, all the way to our town, the little hamlets and farms around it. We see the sand dunes, the church tower and the windmill from our neighboring town, and when you look down from here, a little to the left, you can see Opa and Oma Jansen's house.

We eat our sandwiches, and we talk and we kiss. It all seems so right!

Peter puts his arm around me when we walk home, and with the other arm he swings the empty basket. Once and a while we stop for another kiss.

A threesome of Germans cyclist comes our way when we walk back into town. One of them is Werner Scarcheek!

"Hubba, hubba!" he yells, and makes an obscene gesture.

"Just smile, Mieneke," Peter says under his breath and, with a big grin on his face, he moves us over to let the soldiers go through.

Finally we get our test results and go to the school to pick up our diplomas. We've all passed, even Peer, who missed a lot of classes because of his father's injuries. We're goofy and giddy on the way home.

"We should have a celebration!" Margie says. "Let's have a party! We should invite a whole bunch of people and rent the old gym!"

"That wouldn't go over very well with the Germans, Margie, but we could have it in our back yard, maybe?"

"Why don't we have a hay-ride?" Peer says. "Pa would let us use the horse and wagon. It'll be fun, but there's only enough room for our own group and Tom and Ina, if you want to ask them. We could go over the heather field to the sand dunes."

"Peer, you're a genius! We can all bring something to eat and have a picnic!"

"Let's do it this Saturday afternoon at one o'clock? Peter, could you come around ten and help decorate the wagon?"

"Yes, and can everybody bring some food?"

We are having a party!

Ma and Aunt Jenny are in the backyard. It's a nice sunny day, and they're enjoying a cup of tea on the patio, while sorting out vegetable seeds.

After they admire my diploma Ma says, "A letter came for you today, Mieneke; it's from Hanna! It's on the kitchen table." My heart skips a few beats when I see the letter placed against the vase on the table, and I recognize Hanna's neat, tiny handwriting immediately.

I settle myself in Pa's chair and look at the letter. I'm nervous and carefully open the envelope.

A small note is folded inside the letter.

> To Mieneke Jansen.
> Dear Mieneke,
>
> I've tried many times to send this letter but, until now, nobody ever came by that's going your way. I hope you find this letter in good health.

May 14, 1943.
Dear Mieneke,

I miss you so much, and think about you every day!
I wonder if you had any news about my family—I
of course didn't, and I'm so worried about them
all the time. I pray and ask that they're safe.

It was so hard to leave on that horrible day. I was so
scared! The lady, Sylvia, was very nice and that helped
a lot! There was an older couple with us. They didn't
have an I.D card, so we could only travel at night. It
was hard and it rained every day. Most days we were so
cold and our feet were wet all the time it seemed.

The older woman with us complained a lot and after a while
she drove me nuts! She got us in danger a few times, because
she couldn't shut up. We were chased by some farm dogs one
day and she kept yelling! Sylvia grabbed her and pushed her
down. Sylvia was mad! She covered the woman's mouth and
told her to be quiet! She could have gotten us all killed! She
complained about the food too! I had to laugh when Sylvia
said: "Eat! You're not at the Hilton!" She ate the same as we
did, after a few days on the road, once she was hungry enough!

During the day, we rested. We slept in barns, on straw bales
or in the hay loft and covered ourselves with horse blankets.
I'm grateful for the people who helped us and brought us food.
One family let us sleep in real beds, and we had a meal at the
kitchen table. That was so good! Often we had to find our way
off the beaten path and a few times, we had to wade through
creeks and go through very dense bush, but we made it! After
about a week on the road, we came to the farm in Friesland,
our final destination! Sien and Niels Bouwsma are wonderful
people. They have (can you believe it!) ten grown-up children.
I had a hard time understanding them at first, but now I'm
getting used to the Frisian language. The children come over
often and they're very nice too! Those are happy days. They all
play music and we sing along. We play shuffleboard and card
games. Too bad we have to hide when the little grandchildren
are here, but it's a bit too risky, as they might talk! Sien—they
insist we call them by their first names—teaches me how
to crochet. She has a huge basket full with scrap wool. I'm
making a blanket in many colors, just for you! (Ha, ha!) There
is another boy here now. He came a few days after I did. His
name is Arie Sanders, and he's Jewish too. I like him. He's cute

and funny and makes me laugh when I'm sad. He reminds me of Davie. I read a lot. Sien has so many books! And I'm allowed to read whatever I want, after my chores are done!

The farm is about one kilometer away from the main road, which runs along a dike. We can see anybody coming! When we go outside, we have to stay behind the house and the barns or else we will be seen. One day we had a terrible scare. Niels saw a German car drive up. He quickly took us to the back and into the pig-pen. He had dug a hole underneath the floor and we had to lower ourselves down through the hatch, and Niels covered it with straw. It is small down there and it stank so badly! We were in there for a while, hours it seemed; our legs cramped up and we were so cold! We could hear the pig snorting and scraping above us and I was so frightened! After a while Niels lifted the lid and we crawled out. I was so happy to be able to stretch my legs again! The soldiers came for chickens. Niels told them he doesn't keep chickens over the winter. Sien offered them a loaf of bread and some cream, which they took. It was a good thing they didn't snoop around the farm. They would have found the pig!

You must be done school soon. Please keep all your notes and I can use them to catch up. There isn't much more to tell you. I don't know if you're able to write me back. I will try to get a letter to you again. I do hope we will see each other soon! The war will end!

"This too shall pass."

I read that in one of Sien's books. I believe Solomon said it and Abraham Lincoln used it in one of his speeches, apparently! So it must be good and it's now my favorite quote!

Please give my love to our friends. I miss them too, and hope they're all doing well. And thank your parents for helping me—I love them

I miss you, Mieneke, and I love you, your friend forever!! Hanna.

I take a deep breath and choke back my tears. *Oh Hanna! I miss you so much!* I read the letter again, and slowly I fold it and put it back in the envelope.

Ma comes into the kitchen and sits on the armrest.

"Are you okay? How is Hanna?"

Astrid Zoer

"Hanna is doing fine Ma, she's with good decent people, like you said, and she sends us all her love. Do you know the people who delivered her letter? I would like to write her, and was wondering if they could take it to her?"

"I don't know who they are unfortunately; they were just passing through. Maybe Pa knows. I'll ask him, but don't get your hopes up, sweetheart. People usually don't like taking anything, unless it's very important, but we'll ask your father."

I get my food basket ready for the picnic and, before I leave the house, I put Hanna's letter in my coat pocket.

Peter comes over as soon as he sees me drive up and gives me a quick kiss when he takes the basket from me.

"You should see the wagon, Mieneke, it's real nice! We worked on it for hours!"

The wagon is absolutely beautiful! The sides are decorated with fir and holly branches. Colorful paper flowers and streamers are pinned in between. A big blue and yellow sign covers the entire backside.

"*CONGRATULATIONS TO OUR STUDENTS*" it reads.

"We would have liked to decorate in the Dutch colors—red, white and blue, and use orange streamers—but that would have caused some trouble, for sure!" Peer says.

Along the insides of the wagon, straw bales make for comfortable seats and there's enough room in the front for our baskets.

The big Belgium horse is harnessed in and ready to go. His blond manes are brushed, and paper flowers are braided all along the thick flaxen tail. The friendly animal seems to know how handsome he looks and patiently waits for his passengers to take their seats. He ripples his shiny coat and whips his tail across the flanks to chase the pesky flies away. Then he whinnies, and scrapes his hoof impatiently in the gravel, as to say, "Hurry up already! I've waited long enough! Let's go!"

We all climb into the wagon. After we've taken a seat, Peer, with a click of his tongue, orders the horse in motion, and we're on our way. Peer's family waves until we're out of sight, calling out, "Have fun!"

"Let's go through town first before we head out to the dunes, Peer."

We're filled with joy and want everybody to see the decorated wagon. People stop on the street and come out of their house to watch our happy parade go by, and children run behind the wagon. Everybody waves and yells, "Congratulations!"

Two soldiers step off their bikes, tip their hat and smile.

"You're suckers!" Tom says under his breath, while smiling.

"Please Tom, stop that! Not all of them are bad!" Margie says.

Opa, Oma, Aunt Jenny, Uncle Jan and Margie's Ma are waiting in front of my grandparent's house to cheer us on. Opa holds up his hand and we stop. He walks around the wagon to do an inspection. "Good job, boys!"

He takes an apple out of a bag and feeds it to the horse. He hands the bag to Peer.

"There should be enough apples for all of you. Have fun and be careful!"

We turn into a sandy road, and soon find ourselves in the midst of flowering heather fields guarded by groups of columned junipers. White poplars and Scotch pines provide cool shady spots. The air is heavy with the sweet scent of the purple fields. Butterflies flutter from one flower to the next and buzzing bees forage for honey. Cute little rabbits, nibbling on heather roots, quickly scurry into their burrows when our noisy group comes too close.

We agree to stop near a large sandy hollow, and Peer ties the reins to a low-hanging tree branch.

"I brought a volleyball set—let's set up the net and have a game!" Peter says. "The boys will play against the girls!"

"Well, that should be an easy victory for us ladies!" Ina says. "Let's do it!"

Nobody takes the game very seriously. We're goofy and tease each other, and after a while Tom says: "That's enough of that. I'm hungry—let's eat!"

We unload the baskets and spread our food on a tablecloth. There's so much food! Cheese, sausages, bread, jams and fruit!

The afternoon would have been perfect if Hanna was here too. I let the warm, fine sand run through my bare toes and think about her. I miss her so much! I remember the afternoon when Hanna and I were making sandcastles in this very same spot, scooping the sand in little yellow pails with Oma's old spoons.

"It would have been so nice if Hanna was here with us today," I say.

"She's been on everybody's mind I believe. I've been thinking about her a lot lately," Peer says.

"Did you ever hear from her, Mieneke?"

"It's been over a year, but I received a letter a few days ago, on the day we got our diplomas actually."

"Oh, my God, that was meant to be—it's like a present!" Ina says.

I hand Peter the letter and ask him to read it out loud. We're all quietly thinking about Hanna after he's finished reading her letter.

"It's sure good to know she's safe and with good people," Tom says after a while.

"Yes, you're right, Tom, thank God for that, but I know she wouldn't want us to be all sad and gloomy—she would want us to celebrate!

"Guys, look and see what our mother stuffed in the basket before we left!" Margie says. She takes two jars with cherries in brandy from her basket.

"Ma said to congratulate all of you, and a toast to each and every one!"

We lift our cups. "Here's a toast to us, a toast to Hanna, and a toast to sweet Vrouw Tiemen! Hear, hear!"

We eat, we drink and laugh. We recall all the funny stories from our high school days and the boys tell jokes.

The sun is already going down and Peer says: "All aboard! This is a hay-ride!"

"Let me take the reins for a while, Peer, if that's okay with you?"

"Fine with me Peter, but no hanky-panky. Keep the wagon between the ditches!" Peer says when he sees me take the seat beside Peter.

CHAPTER 9

Uncle Jan didn't come home. It's already eight in the morning and he's still not back! This never happened before—he's always home before daylight.

Aunt Jenny is so worried and keeps calling from the phone at the lock.

"Something has happened to him. I can feel it—something bad has happened; he should be home by now. He should have been home hours ago!"

Cor Dekker and Uncle Jan went to deliver food to the hiding places in the woods, like they've done so many times before, but this time they didn't make it back.

Anneke and I are supposed to get supplies from the city this morning, but I don't know what to do. Is it safe to go? Or should we wait till we know what has happened?

"Maybe I should stay home, Ma, and wait until we know more. I hate to leave now."

"Yes, wait till your father comes home; he should be back any minute now; maybe he's found out where they are."

My father comes home from his morning visit with Opa and Oma. He looks worried and upset.

"Jan was arrested during the night. Cor is at my parent's house. He got there in the middle of the night. He had left earlier to deliver the supplies, and Jan was to drop food at the hiding place closer to town. When Cor came back, he heard voices and yelling on the road ahead. He dropped his bike into the ditch and crawled through the bushes to see what the hell was going on. He saw the Germans, the guys from the city, interrogating Jan, right there on the road. Cor went around them, crossed the heather field and came through the back to my parent's house. Opa told him to stay until it's safe to leave. The Germans patrolled the edge of the woods all night, my father said, hoping to catch somebody coming out of the woods, no doubt. I don't know if they found out what we've been up to or if we were seen by somebody. I don't know what's going on. Why were the Germans there that time of the night? You'd better give Jenny a call, Anna. She should be here."

Anneke is here to pick me up and Aunt Jenny walks in at the same time.

"Are you ready, Mieneke? What's going on?"

"I think we should lay low for a few days, until we know more. We don't know what the Nazis have found out or if it was just a coincidence, which I doubt it was," Pa says, after he tells Anneke and Aunt Jenny about Uncle Jan's arrest.

"Mieneke, go to Vrouw Dekker and tell her what happened, and that Cor is safe. He should be home around four. I told Oma to bike home with him later this afternoon. Hank, you'll cover for me at the plant, and I'll go to the hotel to find out what's going on with Jan."

"I'm coming with you," Aunt Jenny says, and puts on her coat.

"It's better that I go alone, Jenny. I'll be back as soon as I can. Just hang in there girl, and wait here at home with Anna and the girls."

Peter is still home, and opens the door as soon as he sees me drive up. He looks drawn and worried. He grabs my hand.

"Have you heard anything? My father didn't come home last night."

I put my arms around him.

"Peter it is okay, your father is safe at my grandparent's home."

"Thank God! Please, sweetheart, come in."

Vrouw Dekker sits at the table. She looks tired and pale, as if she hasn't slept all night.

"Meneer Dekker will be home this afternoon Vrouw Dekker. He's at my Opa and Oma's, but Uncle Jan was arrested. Pa is at the hotel now to talk to the Germans. Hopefully we'll know more in a few hours."

"Thank God! Thank you, Mieneke, for letting us know—but poor Jenny! She must be devastated!"

"Yes, she's taking it very hard. All we can do now is wait. Maybe the Germans will let him go after my father talks to them."

"I'll pray for that! Peter, you can go to work now. I'll be alright."

"Get some sleep Ma, you've got a few hours before Pa comes home; you look exhausted."

"I'll try, son."

"You promise?"

"I promise—you go, Peter."

"I'm so worried Peter. What happens if my Pa can't take Uncle Jan home?"

"Your Pa is a good talker. If anybody can do it, he's the one. Let's go—I'll take you home, but then I have to go to the farm. I promised Peer that I'd help him today."

"Somebody must have seen Uncle Jan when he went to the hiding place. How else could the Germans have known he was there? If they also know where the hiding place is, then the people there are in danger, too. What do we do? Maybe we should go and warn them before it's too late."

"No, sweetheart, we have to wait. We can't do anything on our own. I'll be back soon, and I'll tell Peer what happened. He'll understand. We can do the work tomorrow. I'll come back as soon as I can, okay?"

When I come around the corner, I meet up with Opa.

"Is there any news, Opa?"

"I'm on the way to your house to find out."

Paul de Wal is just leaving our house. "It doesn't look good, Jochem. You'd better go inside and talk to Martin. I'll be back later. We have to find a way to get to the hiding place and get the men out. The Germans are up to no good. How much do they know? We can't take any chances. Damn! This is a tricky situation!"

Aunt Jenny is in Pa's chair, wrapped in a blanket. Her eyes are red and swollen from crying.

"I'm going to the hotel. I have to see Jan, I can't just sit here!"

"Jenny you can't, we have to wait! I'll go again first thing in the morning. You can't go there now, you'll only make things worse," Pa says.

"So Martin, what did they tell you, how did it go? Did you see Jan?" Opa asks, before he sits down.

"It's not good Pa. Jan, of course, didn't have a good enough reason or excuse why he was there with food and supplies in his bag. Jan told them he had gone shopping earlier in the city and decided to take the road through the forest, to look for blueberries before going home, and he had lost track of the time, but the Germans didn't buy that story. I told them Jan is needed at the lock, but they just laughed at that. If he would tell them the truth and tell them if anybody else was with him, they would let him go. Of course Jan didn't tell them anything. He doesn't believe they would let him go, no matter what he tells them."

"The Germans asked me to talk to Jan, to talk some sense into him, they said. They put Jan and me alone in a room. Jan told me the same story. We knew they were listening!

"They'll keep him locked up at the hotel overnight and take him to the city tomorrow. Kaiser, the head guy here in town, said to come back tomorrow morning. Kaiser is not so bad really. He would have let Jan go home I believe, but the Nazis from the city are ruthless and determined to keep him locked up. There's not much Kaiser can do on his own. If they take Jan tomorrow, Kaiser will let me know where they'll take him. Let's hope it doesn't come to that. All we can do now is wait and pray."

"We should tell the Germans why Jan was there!" says Jenny. "Why should he be locked up and others go free? It's just not right. I want my husband to come home!"

"Jenny, don't say that," Opa says with a stern voice. "You know Jan wouldn't want you to do that. He would have talked himself if he thought it would do any good. What we do is illegal; you'll get everybody arrested—including yourself—and it will not bring Jan home. He wants you to be strong and carry on. He'll be home again, God willing, when the time comes. Keep your chin up, girl. We're all here for you! I'd better go home. Oma is worried and needs to know what's going on. Let me know right away if you hear anything."

"I should go to the plant and see how Hank is getting on. We'll be back for supper," says Pa.

"Mieneke, why don't you and Anneke take Aunt Jenny home? Jenny, you could stay here. The girls can go to your house with you and pack a few clothes if you like," Ma asks.

"Yes, I rather not stay home by myself—thank you, Anna."

"Do you think there's still a chance that Uncle Jan will come home, Papa?" I ask my father during dinner.

"I hope so, but all we can do now is hope for the best. I'll talk to Kaiser first thing in the morning."

"I'll cover for you at the plant again, Father," says Hank.

We all go to bed early that night.

The following morning, before I come downstairs, my father already returned from the hotel. He looks tired.

"They took him away. I was there just in time to say goodbye. He told me to tell Jenny to be strong. He will send word, if he can, as soon as possible."

Pa puts his elbows on the table. With a sorrowful look, he places his head in his hands. "They did a number on him Anna, trying to beat out of him what they want to know. He looked so beaten up! My God, give me strength! What is this world coming to, and when will this misery ever end?"

My father gets up from the table. I feel so bad for him. I can see how frustrated and angry he is.

"Is there anything I can do, Father?"

"Not now, Mieneke. I have to go to Opa and Oma and give them the bad news. I, as sure as hell, hoped to be able to tell them anything better than this. I will go back to the hotel and see if Kaiser knows where Jan will be taken. I'll be home a little later for supper, Anna. I have to talk to Dekker after work."

"Kaiser told me Jan has been transferred to a camp in near Osnabruck, Germany," Pa says, when he comes home in the evening.

"Kaiser almost seemed sorry for Jan's arrest. He said if Jenny writes letters to Jan, he'll try to get them delivered, but he can't promise anything. He apologized that he couldn't stop the transport, but he has to follow orders. In any case, there's nothing we can do, but at least we know where Jan is. We have to carry on. We can't let those bastards beat us down!"

Jenny is inconsolable and rolls herself in the blanket. She lays down on the sofa in the front room and doesn't talk to anybody.

We're uncertain why the Nazis were there at that time in the evening when they arrested Uncle Jan. How much do they know? Was it a coincidence? And if it wasn't, who is the informer? We can't take any chances.

Opa and Oma go for a walk in the woods to warn the people in hiding and tell them they have to move to a different location. They agree on a spot where to hide a map with the location of their new hiding place.

Aunt Jenny finally gets up and off the sofa and writes a letter to Uncle Jan. She and Ma walk to the hotel and hand the letter to Kaiser, who promises to do his best to have the letter delivered.

When Opa comes to the house the following afternoon to go over the map with father, he says: "That was a close call, Martin, but we know now who the traitor is!" When he and Oma went for their walk to pick up the map, they heard an army vehicle come up the road.

"Thank God we were off the path, and they didn't see us."

Opa told Oma to hide further into the woods, and he went through the bush to have a closer look. He saw two German officers and Geert Dolsman, who works for an N.S.B. farmer.

"When you look across the east side of the path, there's an opening in the forest, just wide enough to have a clear view of his house, which is at the edge of the cow pasture. He must have seen us coming and going, and he must be the one who reported it, to get brownie points with the boss, no doubt," Opa says.

"The Nazis parked the vehicle and walked straight to where the men were hiding before. Thank God they found it empty! We have to stay away from that route and find a way to get around it. Also, I believe, we shouldn't take the supplies straight to the hiding places anymore, but hide the food away from them, in a different spot. Oma and I will go for a little hike again tomorrow and map something out."

Opa gets up and before he leaves he says, "Tell Peter to come here the day after tomorrow at six, and Mieneke, you have to be here too—and so should you, Hank."

"Are you coming downstairs now, Mieneke? Opa is here and Peter should be here any minute," Pa calls from the bottom of the stairs.

I put my book away, and hear Peter come in when I go down the stairs. We gather in the secret room.

"We decided to throw the Germans off by sending a young couple on the food run this time. The Germans might still patrol the area after Jan's arrest. Are you up to this, Mieneke?"

"Yes, of course I am—I want to do this for sure!"

"Okay Hank, please open the map, and we'll show Mieneke and Peter the route, and where to drop the supplies."

Pa points at the map.

"The first location is here. In order to get there, you have to follow this path. We abandoned the old route for obvious reasons. This path runs parallel to the creek. It's narrow and harder to bike on, so be careful and don't go too fast. We opted for this route, because there's a wide strip of dense shrubbery blocking the view from the main road.

"When you come to the end, you'll see a fork in the road. There's a marker pointing to the Moor. You both know where that is. Follow the path, for about a hundred meters, and you'll see a tall old tree on the left, about thirty steps off the path. You can't be seen from the path, but be very quiet, so nobody can hear you.

"Lightning split the bottom of the trunk a few years ago, and in between the split, Opa dug a hole and covered it with a wooden plank. Remove the leaves and the dirt from the plank, and you'll find a rope. Pull the rope and it'll bring the plank up. Hide the food and cover the hole with leaves and dirt again.

"There's a short, thick stick on the ground beside the tree. Put it up against the tree and the men will know the supplies are there. You take it from here, Pa."

Opa turns the map toward him.

"Next, you'll follow the path here," he says, and he traces the route with his pencil. "It veers off, but comes around to the marker which points to the sheepfold.

"We used to go there to see the newborn lambs, remember, Mieneke? You know where it is too, don't you, Peter?" When Peter nods, Opa goes on. "Go around the shepherd's shed to the back where the well is. It's not in use anymore, and it's partially filled with rocks and dirt; there is, however, enough room left on the top to hide the supplies. If the lid is up, drop the supplies, and make sure to close the lid. When the lid is closed, it's a sign the supplies have been delivered."

Opa gives the map back to Father.

"You'll show them what else they need to know, Martin," he says.

"Here, where you see this small red dot, is the hiding place. It's about half a kilometer north of the well. The first hiding place, the one by the tree, is here. If you follow this path and you go in this way, for about four hundred meters, you'll find them there. You don't go there of course, but it's good to know where they are. Now you both know where this is, don't you? Look at the map again; study it if you have to. You can't take the map with you!"

"I know exactly where it is, Meneer Jansen," Peter says.

"So do I, Pa. I don't need to study the map. I know exactly where to go."

"Okay, then. You'll go to Opa and Oma on Saturday afternoon, the supplies will be there, and it's where you'll load your bags."

We're at my grandparents' house the following Saturday at one thirty. Opa already sorted the groceries, and it doesn't take long to pack the bags.

"Please come here first before you go home. I want to know you're safe. Oh dear, we shouldn't have agreed to this, you're both too young!"

"Don't worry, Oma, we'll be fine; we'll come back as soon as we're done."

I'm nervous and pretend this is just an ordinary afternoon bike-ride.

The path is as narrow and bumpy as we were told, and doesn't seem to be biked on very often, if ever at all! I follow Peter, who gives me a signal every time there's a rut, a hump or a protruding tree root.

Pa directions are easy to follow and, after about forty five minutes, we put the lid on the well at the second drop-off, and decide to take the easier path back home. I'm so relieved we're done! It's like a weight has been lifted off my shoulders. "Phew, I'm glad that's done and over with!"

"Yes, that was tense, but somebody has to do it. You did good, sweetheart. Come here!"

Peter takes me in his arms and gives me a long, lingering kiss. His hard, muscled body tightly against mine sends a tingle to my stomach and a hot throbbing pulse spreads down into my loins. I love him so much! I want more, and I can feel he does too, but we can't go any further!

"Oh dear, we'd better stop now, Peter!"

I take a deep breath and, although I want him so much, I take a step back.

He lingers a bit, but slowly takes his lips from mine and loosens his embrace.

"We can't Peter, we can't go any further. I know others our age do, but what if I became pregnant? We're too young, and besides, I wouldn't want to bring a baby into this crazy world, would you?"

"No, dear God, no! I'm sorry —you're right and I know, I know, but jeez, it's not easy is it?"

"It sure isn't!"

I put my arms around him and kiss him again.

"Let's stop at Oma's for a bite to eat."

CHAPTER 10

January 1944 – December 1944

Peter is helping Peer Winters on the farm and I keep myself busy with the garden and house chores, but there's only so much to do. I find myself getting more bored with each passing day. Once and a while I'll get together with Margie, but she is busy studying her father's books. She's determined to be ready for college, as soon as that day comes. I look for work around town, but nobody is hiring these days.

One afternoon, when I come home from Margie's, the local nurse, Vrouw Kamp, who's called Sister Kamp by everybody, is visiting with Ma.

"I actually came to see you, Mieneke," she says. "I'm looking for somebody to give me a hand. There just aren't enough hours in the day to visit all my patients. I was thinking of you. Would you be interested in working with me? The hours are long some days, and it doesn't pay a heck of a lot, but I believe you'll find it very rewarding."

"I would love to, Sister, but do you think I qualify? I have never done anything like it before."

"I would train you, of course, and you only have to look after the less demanding patients. All you have to do is bring the medication around, change dressings, help some of the people with their bath now and again, and check on their wellbeing on a regular basis. How about it, Mieneke, would you give it a try?"

I agree to the job, and after Sister Kamp takes me on her route for a few weeks, I'm working by myself. I love my work. The people on my route are always happy to see me and spoil me, whenever they can, with gifts of homemade bread, jams and preservatives, which I often pass on to the less fortunate. As an added bonus, I get to see Peter more often, since I have to visit Peer's father at least once a week.

I have to see Vrouw Oost, who gave birth to her sixth baby. She had a difficult delivery this time around, during which she lost a lot of blood. Her two older daughters look after the house, and mind the little ones while their mother is taking a week-long bed rest, ordered by the sister.

When I ride up to the house, I see a German jeep parked near the barn. I wonder if I should come back later, but that would mean that I have to make an extra trip the next day. I decide to stop in anyways and see how the family is getting on.

I lean my bike against the wall near the door and, when I'm just about to knock, I hear loud voices coming from the kitchen. Children cry. I open the door just enough to peek inside.

Two German soldiers stand in the kitchen. A kitchen chair is tipped over and broken teacups are scattered over the floor.

One of the soldiers grabs the oldest girl by her long hair, twists it around his hand, and yanks her head back. With his face an inch away from hers, he shouts, "Where is your brother? Why didn't he report at the office? He had better report tonight before eight or we will come back and take you instead!"

I almost turn around to get on my bike and get the hell out of here as fast as I can, but I can't—instead I open the door wider and step inside. The soldier turns around and my heart drops when I see Werner Zimmerman's face.

"Well, well, look who's here! What the hell do you want," he sneers at me.

"I've come to see Vrouw Oost," I say, as assertively as I can.

"You'd better leave, unless you can tell me where that waste of a skin son of her is!"

"We don't know where my son is. We haven't seen him for over a week. I was hoping you knew and came with news about his whereabouts," Vrouw Oost says.

"You stupid woman—you're a liar, and liars should be punished!" he yells.

He grabs her throat and pushes her against the wall, turns to grab a kitchen chair, swings it over his head, but when he's about to is strike her, I quickly step between him and Vrouw Oost and spread my arms wide to protect her.

"Please, stop! Can't you see she's sick! You're scaring the little ones!"

"Get out of my way, you little bitch!"

He brings the chair up higher and is about to bring it down hard, when his tall companion grabs his arm and pulls it down.

"That's enough, Zimmerman. That's enough! Let's get out of here."

The chair clatters on the floor.

Scarcheek walks to the door, but before he leaves the room, he kicks the chair, turns around and, with spit in the corners of his mouth, screams: "You'd better tell that piece of garbage son of yours to report first thing in the morning!"

"Hush now, sweetheart, hush," I say when I pick up one of the crying boys. The tall solder, seemingly lost, is watching us. He walks over and strokes the little boy's hair. I can see tears in his friendly blue eyes; he looks so sad.

"I'm so sorry. I really am. I have little ones at home. I haven't seen them for so long and I miss them so much, and all this for a bloody war. Why, what for?"

He abruptly turns around and, softly closing the door behind him, he leaves.

I ask one of the girls to put the kettle on and send the boy outside to get a loaf of bread and a jar of jam from my bag. We tidy up the kitchen and sweep the floor.

"Are you all right, Vrouw Oost? Come sit down with us, and we'll have a nice cup of tea. It'll be good for you to get up for a little while."

I act calm and collected, but inside I'm still shaking when I sit down.

It starts to rain outside.

One of the little boys presses his nose against the window.

"April flowers bring May flowers," he says, and wipes his tears with the cuff of his sleeve.

We all start to laugh.

CHAPTER 11

Peter races up the gravel path, throws his bike against the wall and runs into the kitchen. "Have you heard the news?" he says. "The Allied troops have invaded Italy and captured Rome. Oh dear God, they're finally coming this way! I can't believe it Mieneke, we will be free soon!"

After we hear the rumors that our liberators are on the way, we make sure there's always one of us in the meeting room, in case there's a radio broadcast.

Finally, on June 6, 1944, we hear the news on BBC.

"D-Day has come. Early this morning, the Allies began the assault on the North-Western face of Hitler's European fortress.

The first official news came just after half-past nine. Under the command of General Eisenhower, Allied forces, supported by strong air forces, began landing on the northern coast of France."

We cry and laugh at the same time. We're so excited! Soon the war will be over! Peter and I spread the European map on the floor and mark our liberators' progress in red ink. Shortly after the invasion of Normandy, Paris is liberated.

The red line continues!

A few weeks after our exciting news, Peter and I are on the path to the first food drop-off, when I spot a patch of chanterelles on a mossy slope underneath a tall Pine tree. "Let's take this path back Peter and we can pick those mushrooms."

"Yes—I like chanterelles fried with a little parsley. Mmm, yes, yummy!"

We're back at the spot after forty five minutes and pick all the mushrooms we can find. We fill half a basket with the golden yellow chanterelles and also find enough blueberries for at least half a dozen jars with jam! This is our lucky day!

We rest in the sun on a soft mossy patch. It's so quiet and peaceful here. All we hear is the melodic chirps of forest birds and the lazy humming of insects. From the distance, the hammering of a busy woodpecker laboring for his grub adds rhythm to nature's concert. The forest is filled with soft soothing music, just for Peter and me, or so it seems.

"Listen...did you hear that?"

"Yes, it's a woodpecker."

"No, no, not that. Hush...Listen...listen again."

And then I hear it too—the low rumbling sound of a heavy vehicle's engine. When it gets louder, Peter says, "That's a German truck!"

He jumps up, but crouches down again and crawls across the path, slides through the ditch and, keeping his body low, moves through the shrubbery to the main path, where the sound is coming from.

I can hear voices now, and quickly hide behind a bush, just in case.

Peter is back in a few minutes.

"Hide my bike underneath that bush in the ditch, go to your grandparent's house and wait for me there. I have to warn the men. I believe they've been found out."

"But Peter—"

"Do it, Mieneke, go now!" Keeping his head down, he zigzags through the dense woods and is gone.

I ride to my grandparent's house as fast as I can, but I take the narrow path too fast and don't notice the tree root sticking out of the ground. I flip head over heels and when I land in the muddy ditch, I cut my knee on a sharp edged rock. A fierce pain shoots through my leg and I clasp my knee in agony. I almost cry and fear that I can't stand up! It's hard to bend my knee, but I do get back on my bike. I'm bleeding, my front wheel is bent and wobbles, but I ignore it and keep going as fast as I can.

I enter the garden through the berry bushes, and when I come through the gate by the rabbit cages, I see Opa on the bench by the holly hedge, smoking his pipe.

"Mieneke, girl, you startled me. What on earth happened to you, and where is Peter?"

"Opa, the Nazis were there. Peter is warning the men. I fell and hurt my knee."

"My dear child, we'd better go in and have Oma look after that cut!"

"O my goodness dear, you're bleeding! Come here. We have to wash the mud off your legs to see how bad it is."

The cold pump-water hurts when it runs over my leg, but it seems to slow down the bleeding.

"Jochem dear, get the peroxide off the shelf, and bring some strips of cotton from the basket. There, there, it's clean. You really got a nasty cut sweetheart, but there's no dirt in it, thank goodness. This peroxide is going to sting a bit, Mieneke, are you ready?"

I brace myself for more pain, and it does sting. Oma helps me to the kitchen and sits me down on a chair. Opa puts another chair underneath my leg and pours me a cup of coffee. Oma wraps cotton strips around my knee, and when she's finished, they both pull up a chair and sit down, anxious to hear what happened.

"So, tell us now, what in the world happened? Is Peter okay?"

"I don't know exactly what to tell you; it all went so fast. We heard a German truck, Peter had a look, and when he came back, told me to hide his bike, and to go home and wait. He said he had to warn the men. Oh please, I hope he's alright!"

Just as I finish my sentence, Peter walks into the kitchen. His clothes are torn and deep, bleeding scratches cover his arms and legs.

"Oh Peter, you're here, I was so worried! Are you alright, and were you there in time?"

He bends over and kisses me.

"I'm fine sweetheart, just a few scratches, but look at you, you're hurt!"

"Let me have a look at those cuts, Peter. We'd better get you out of these clothes," Oma says, and takes Peter to the pump.

She hands him a pair of Opa's pants and a clean shirt.

Peter rolls up the sleeves, which are too short, and laughs when Oma starts fussing over his pants, which are too short also.

"Don't worry Oma. Nobody will look at my pants!"

"Please tell us, son, what was going on there in the woods? Mieneke said you ran to warn the men."

"Yes. When we heard the truck, I crawled through the bushes to see what the Germans were up to. A group of soldiers jumped out of the back and lined up. In the front of the line, I saw a couple of city officers, and Kaiser was there talking to the Mayor. That Mayor is a dirty traitor, I can tell you that. He pointed straight to where the hiding spot is. How in the world did he find out where the men are hiding? I don't understand it—somebody must be talking, or is spying on us. In any case, I figured out what they were up to, and I started to run as fast as I could, hoping to outrun the Nazis and get there in time to warn the men."

"And did you, Peter? Did you get there in time, and did they get away?"

"I sure hope so, Opa. I quickly helped them to get some of their things out, but I didn't hang around. I just kept running. I did hear shouting, but no gunshots.

I do hope they ran fast enough and got away."

"Oh dear God, let's pray they did, and be thankful the two of you made it home safe. Maybe you should stay here tonight. It might be safer. I'll go to your parents and let them know where you are."

"We should be okay, Oma. It's still early and I don't believe they're looking for us; there's no reason why they would. We'll go straight home, don't worry."

"I have to sit on your back seat, Peter. My wheel was damaged when I fell, and my knee feels stiff now; it might be too painful to bike."

"Leave your bike here and I'll fix it for you tomorrow," Opa says.

"I've lost the chanterelles and the berries, Peter." I tell him on the way home.

"Oh well, if wasn't for those mushrooms, we would have taken the regular path back and run into the Germans. We'll go for a walk when your knee has healed and pick some more."

"I was so worried, Peter, and so scared, I wouldn't know what to do, if something had happened to you!"

He turns around to look at me and smiles.

"It's alright now, sweetheart. I can outrun those fat Germans any day!"

He always knows how to make me laugh.

"Keep your eyes on the road, Peter; we got hurt once already today and that's enough, don't you think?"

"Yes Ma'am! I'll drop you off and go straight home. I wouldn't mind getting out of these clothes!"

He gives me a quick kiss before he gets back on the bike.

I start to laugh again.

"Now you're laughing at me?"

"Sorry, but I can't help it, you look so cute on your mother's bike and in my Opa's pants!"

"I'm leaving before anybody else sees me in these clothes! Look after your leg sweetheart. I'll see you tomorrow."

He waves before he turns around the corner.

This time it's my mother and Aunt Jenny who take a walk in the forest. They find the hole under the tree empty. At least the men got the supplies. When Ma lowers the plank, Jenny notices the tip of a piece of paper sticking out from underneath a rock in the hole. "We're okay," it reads, and on the other side somebody drew a crude map.

Pa and Hank study the map that evening, and the following day Opa finds the new hiding place far into the dense forest. That's when he hears from the men how two of them were shot in the head after being interrogated by the Nazis.

"We ran, after Peter came to warn us, but Harm van Dijk couldn't run fast enough. His brother tried to pull him along, but it slowed him down too, and the Nazis caught up with both of them," one of the men says.

"I jumped in the creek and hid underneath a willow bush. I was frightened the Germans would catch me too, and every time when I thought they looked in my direction, I lowered my head underneath the water, but I did see what they did to Harm and his brother. They beat them up so bad! It was horrible to watch. Thank God they didn't talk, and they kept telling them that it was only the two of them hiding there. After about thirty minutes, their hands were tied up behind their back, and I thought they were taken to the truck—that's where they seemed to be heading. One German officer was really pissed off, I could tell, and suddenly he walked up behind them and shot them both in the head, and then ordered the soldiers to drag the bodies to the truck.

"It was terrible and it took a good five minutes before I was able to move. I was in shock I think, and so cold, and couldn't stop crying," the young man tells my grandfather.

"Thank Peter for what he did for us, Jansen. It's horrible what happened, but if it wasn't for Peter, we would all be dead. We do appreciate it; he's a good kid."

"We should have a meeting and see what we can do. We might have to hide the men around town and on the farms. This was the second close call, and two men are dead now. I don't know what's going on or who is talking, but I don't like it one bit," Opa says.

The Canadians, English and Americans join forces and make their way north. They move up through France and Belgium and, in the late summer of 1944, all the southern provinces of the Netherlands are liberated.

We're delirious with happiness and spread the word.

"Did you hear? Were you told? Did you read the paper or listen to the radio? The war will be over by Christmas!"

Unfortunately the Germans don't give up that easy; their resistance is fierce, and soon it's clear to all of us that the war will not end in 1944. Our red line on the map stops.

CHAPTER 12

Autumn is here and, as if touched by a magic wand, the leaves put on a brilliant show of colors. From bright golden yellows to vibrant reds, they transform and proudly exhibit their warm, rich and splendid hues. Children collect the prettiest ones and put the leaves between the pages of heavy books to dry. They gather beech-nuts, strip them of their thorny coats, and thread the little nuts into long necklaces. They make toys and make-believe pipes with the chestnuts, and fill burlap sacks with acorns for pig feed.

The entire forest floor provides a treasure hunt for all.

Soon after I can feel the frost in the air, and I know winter will be early.

The Dutch in the densely-populated provinces above the great rivers are starving. The Germans cut off food and fuel supplies to punish the Dutch citizens for not aiding in the German war effort. Butter is not available at all and animal fats are dwindling. Stamps for meat and dairy products are worthless. Everybody is cold and hungry. People walk tens of kilometers to trade their valuables for food at the farms in the Northern provinces. They come on bikes with garden hoses for tires or no tires at all. Large sacks are carried on their backs and they push strollers and hand-carts. They're hungry and sick and so terribly cold. And that it is the coldest winter we had in decades, is adding to their misery.

It's a miserable afternoon. A strong wind blows from the North. The wet snow and sleet seem to penetrate my skin like hard, sharp needles. I'm glad I only had a few patients today and I get to go home early.

I'm the only one on the road, until I see two figures in the distance. When they come closer, I see an older man and a boy pushing a stroller. They're wet and cold, and look so gaunt and tired. They stop when the man has a coughing spell and I stop too.

"Are you all right? Is there anything I can do for you?"

Before the men can answer he coughs again.

"Sorry, it's just a bad cold, and this weather doesn't help it much, that's for sure!"

"Where are you heading?"

"I don't know. This hasn't been our lucky day. We've been on the road for over a week, unable to find any food. We had a meal or two, but nothing to take home to the wife and my daughter. I'm hoping to find a place for tonight. Maybe that farmer over there will let us sleep in the barn," he says, pointing at van Holt's farm.

"Tomorrow we might have to go further north, but I don't know, it's getting harder and harder."

"Why don't you come home with me first, at least you can have something to eat and warm up before you go on."

"I don't want you to go through any trouble."

"It's no trouble and you have to eat. I'm Mieneke Jansen," I say, and I hold out my hand.

"My name is Bas Boonstra and this is my son Bram. We walked all the way from Haarlem."

Ma opens the porch door when she hears us walk up the gravel path.

I introduce Bas and his son, and quickly explain their situation.

"Come in, come in and warm up. Hand me those wet clothes, they can dry by the fireplace while you have a bite to eat."

Jenny already busies herself with the food, and in no time at all our visitors have a warming bowl of bean soup and a few slices of bread in front of them.

"Now eat it slowly," Jenny says. "Too much food all at once will make you sick."

While savoring his meal, taking a break between each bite, Bas Boonstra starts to talk.

"We came up here to find food, but it's getting really tough. We have to walk so much further now to get anything at all. One day we were lucky and we got a sack with potatoes, a few sugar beets and some vegetables, all of which I traded for my wife's gold chain and my father's silver pocket watch. We were only a few days away from home when we got stopped by German soldiers. They had one look in our stroller, tipped it over and dumped everything into the canal. They yelled and swore at us, "Thieves, you're nothing but thieves! You steal food that should go to the army!"

"It's very bad at home. People strip the wood from empty and bombed houses and steal railroad ties to keep warm and for cooking, if there is anything to cook at all. I stripped my house from all the wood too—there's nothing left. People are dying on the streets. We lost one little girl, she was not even two years old. My wife and our other daughter, little Liselotte, are waiting for us at home. I hope they're okay by themselves. We have been gone for so long. It's horrible back home. People eat anything—tulip bulbs, dogs, cats, and the children lick the empty cans at the soup kitchen. But we have to stay strong. Bram is our oldest boy; he's twelve now and he's a good son," he says and ruffles his son's hair.

Bas starts to cough again.

"Are you okay, Pa?" Bram says, and puts his hand on his father's arm.

"Ja, ja, my son, I'm fine. You eat your soup now."

I get a bottle of cough syrup from my bag and tell Bas to take a spoonful.

"Thank you," he says. "That feels good."

I feel so sorry for these people. The man clearly is sick, and the little boy is so skinny and short for his age; he doesn't look a day older than eight.

Pa and Hank come home for supper and, after being introduced, they sit down with Bas. They talk for a while, and when Bas has another coughing spell, father gets up, takes his coat of the peg and says: "We'd better find you a bed, my friend; you'll need a good night's sleep before you can go on! There's a bed downstairs in the plant where I work. You can bunk there for tonight and we'll see what comes tomorrow."

Bram put his head on the table and is sound asleep.

"Leave your boy with us, Bas. He's exhausted. You can pick him up in the morning. I'll make a bottle of tea and put some bread in the bag too—at least you'll have something for the night," Ma says.

"Thank you so much. I don't have much to pay you with, but what little I've left, I'll give to you," Bas says and reaches in his pocket.

"Put that away Boonstra, there's no need to pay us. We're all in this together and have to look out for each other."

I quickly put the cough syrup in the bag and bring his coat from the front room. "Come along, my man, we just have to go around the corner," Pa says.

We can hear Bas cough again when he and Pa pass the kitchen window. Hank picks up the sleeping boy and puts him in Pa's chair. He puts a pillow under his head and covers him with a blanket.

"Poor little guy," he says and strokes the boy's hair.

"See what those bastards do to us? They starve the people, and make everybody's lives a living hell. And you know why? 'Cause they know their power over us is dwindling. Their enemies are at the doorstep and are closing in, and they know it. That's why they get more miserable and malicious with each passing day. Oh yes, they know it. The war will be over, and the German Reich is crumbling to dust.

The end for them is near!"

Pa is back and he sits down at the table. He rubs his eyes and shakes his head.

"These poor, poor people! It's unbelievable what they have to go through just to stay alive! Let's pray our liberators hurry up before we all starve!"

"Let's leave our bedroom door open, Anna, so we can keep an eye on this little man."

I'd rather starve than eat with your kind! That could very well happen! You're a stupid girl—you might never eat again and you will starve to death.

Scarcheek! His words haunt me.

I'm up early the next morning. Pa left the keys of the plant on the table, and already left for his daily morning visit with Opa and Oma. Hank is downstairs, having his breakfast and making his lunch. "There's coffee on the stove, Mieneke."

Bram stirs and sits up. He wipes the sleep out of his eyes and looks around as if lost.

"Where is my Pa? Did he go and leave me here?"

"No Bram. He didn't leave you here, he's still sleeping. He was very tired last night and so were you; you fell asleep and your father didn't want to wake you. I'm going to get him. Do you want to come, and we'll have breakfast later?"

"Where is he? Why didn't he stay here with me? Where did he go?"

"We don't have a bed for him here, but we do have one downstairs at the plant where Hank and my father work. Here's your coat. Let's go and wake him up."

It's very cold outside, and Hank gets a toque for Bram before we walk to the plant. Hank unlocks the door and Bram and I go down the stairs. Bram runs ahead of me and by the time I get to the room, he's already trying to wake his father.

"Wake up Pa, wake up, we have to go."

His father does not move.

"Pa, get up!"

An eerie feeling comes over me. I kneel down beside Bram and shake Bas Boonstra's arm. He doesn't stir, and when I feel his cold hand I know. I look up at Bram, and when our eyes meet, I know he too realizes that his father is dead.

"Your Pa is gone, Bram."

"No! You're wrong! Pa, wake up!" He flings his body over his father's chest. "Wake up Pa, please, please Pa, don't leave me here by myself, Pa!"

I take his shoulders and gently pull him back.

"Your Pa has passed away, Bram. He was so tired and sick, he needed to rest. He knows you're with good people, Bram."

"No! Get away from me and leave me alone! I will not leave my father. He's not dead!"

Hank comes down the stairs.

"Hurry up, guys. The crew will be here soon!"

He stops when he sees Bas Boonstra's body on the mattress. He takes one more look and kneels down to check the man's pulse.

He looks at Bram and says: "I'm so sorry, Bram, but Mieneke is right—your Papa passed away during the night."

"No! Papa, please!"

He throws his body over his father's again and cries out all of his heartache and pain.

"Let's go home, Bram. Hank will look after your Pa. Don't worry, you'll stay with us. We won't let you go on your own."

Reluctantly he loosens his grip and gets up. I put my arm around his thin, drooping shoulders and gently coach him out of the room. The poor boy keeps looking back at his father until we reach the stairs. There's so much sadness and pain in his eyes that looking at him makes me cry.

Father and Hank take Bas Boonstra to the health care building where, with the help of Sister Kamp, Ma and Aunt Jenny get the body ready for burial.

I find clothes for Bram in the good will box, and he has a bath before putting them on. He sits down in father's chair. He doesn't eat, talk or cry. I wish he would. He just sits there, staring into space. He appears even smaller now than when I first met him. Finally he takes a few little sips of the bouillon I've prepared for him.

"Don't be frightened Bram, you're not alone, and you don't have to leave by yourself. We will look after you. You can stay here until we find your mother. And when we find her, we'll know what to do next."

I keep talking, hoping he will respond and, after I mention his mother, he does, and it almost breaks my heart.

"And what will I tell her when I see her? Tell me, what I should say to my Ma?"

"Bram, this is not your fault; your Pa was very sick. There's nothing you could have done. Your father would have wanted you to be strong and get back to your mother and sister, right?"

He buries his face in his hands and starts to sob.

"Move over a little Bram."

I slide in the chair beside him, pull the blanket over both of us, and with my arms around him, I let him cry until, with his head on my shoulder, he finally falls asleep.

My family and I take Bram to view his father's body. He steps on the footstool in front of the coffin, folds his hands over his father's and prays. He kisses his father's forehead, puts his head on the dead man's chest and cries.

My father stands behind him and, gently taking Bram's arm, he says: "It's all right my boy; your father is at peace now. Let's take him to his resting place, son."

He takes the boy by the hand and leads him outside.

Hank, Peter, Peer, Cor Dekker, Paul de Wal and Margie's brother Tom carry Bas Boonstra to the waiting funeral carriage. They slide the simple pine box inside and close the black curtain.

Walking beside the black horse, Hans Broekman, the undertaker, leads the small, sober funeral procession to the graveyard.

Pastor Strik recites a short but touching sermon, and we sing the beautiful hymn, "Precious Lord, Take My Hand," while the pallbearers lower the casket. Bram looks down on the coffin and with a thin little voice he says, "Goodbye, Papa."

I try not to cry, but when I look at that sad little boy's face, I can't stop the tears from running down my cheeks. Peter squeezes my arm and hands me his handkerchief.

After Pastor Strik says a final prayer, Pa takes one of Bram's hands, my mother takes the other and, taking him between them, they walk Bram home.

Sister Kamp comes to our house after the funeral and collects all of Bas Boonstra's information.

"I will contact the Red Cross in Haarlem as soon as possible, Bram," she says.

"It might be a while until we'll get a reply, but if your Ma is still at the same address, it shouldn't take too long."

"Now, have some of Aunty Jenny's delicious pea soup, Bram. You'll feel a lot better after, I promise." Pa says.

"I will Meneer Jansen."

"Bram, you're part of our family now, and you can call me Uncle Martin—and that's Aunty Anna, okay, my boy? Come on, let's eat."

We enjoy having Bram living with us. Ma's food puts some meat on his bones and after he's gotten healthier, he proves to be very smart and witty.

Hank takes him skating, he goes to "work" on the farm with Peter, and Opa comes by every day to check on him, often taking him home for a sleep-over. Bram enjoys sleeping in the box bed as much as Hanna and I used to.

"It's like sleeping in a big closet, Mieneke!" he says.

Ma checks with the school and, after Bram writes a few tests, he's accepted in the sixth grade, and soon after he starts to act like every other twelve-year-old. Every day after school, he asks if there's any word from his mother, but every day the same answer puts a sad and worried expression on his face.

Finally, Sister Kamp comes by with a letter from Henrika Boonstra.

Inside the envelope are two letters: One for my parents and one for Bram. The letters are written in pencil on the Red Cross' stationary. After Pa reads the letter to himself, he reads it out loud to all of us.

December 8, 1944.

Dear Meneer and Mevrouw Jansen.

First, I want to let you know how grateful I am, and I want to thank you with all my heart for looking after my husband and my boy. They were total strangers to you and you took them in. I'm so grateful!

I don't know how yet, but, God willing, and if he gives me the time, I will pay you back every penny you're out for my husband's funeral and the expenses for my son.

I waited for a long time for Bas and Bram to come home, until I couldn't stay in the house any longer. My daughter and I are in a women's shelter now. It's hard, but at least we have more hands to help with collecting wood and to look for food.

Thank God I had left word with my neighbors, so Bas would be able to find me, in case they came home, or the Red Cross wouldn't have been able to find us. Now, that I'm not waiting any more, I will leave the city as soon as possible. My little girl is getting weaker by the day and I know we might both die of starvation if I don't leave soon. I have relatives in Groningen who would take me in, I believe.

I understand it's a lot to ask, after you have done so much already, but could you please keep my boy until I get there? It should take about a week to walk the distance, and, God willing, we'll be there before Christmas. We will leave tomorrow, after I drop this letter off at the Red Cross' office. I'm nervous and scared, but I have no choice in the matter. I will ask the Lord for his guidance, and if it is His will, then I will hold my boy in my arms again soon. I miss him so much. He's a good boy and he won't cause you any trouble, I promise. Please give him a hug from me, and thank you so much for looking after him. May God bless you; please pray for us.

With my regards,
Henrika Boonstra.

"That poor, poor woman," Ma says. "Life must be a living hell for her! She doesn't have a place to live, she lost her husband and her little girl, and now she could lose her other daughter too—poor soul!"

"She seems determined, though, and certainly hasn't lost her faith. I admire that. I often think there is no God. If there is, He's turned his back on us, and doesn't want anything to do with us. Still, her words give me hope and inspiration, and I will pray for her. I will pray, and I'll ask God to keep her and her daughter safe on this journey, and bring her home to her son and to us."

"I agree, Jenny, and there's no better time than the present. Let's pray."

We all bow our heads and Sister Kamp leads us in prayer.

Bram is so excited when I show him his mother's letter. First his face turns red and then it turns pale. I think he might get sick! He sits down in Pa's chair and slowly reads the letter. He looks up at me and, as his eyes are tearing up, he says, "My mother is coming, she's on her way, and Liselotte is coming too, Mieneke! I have to make sure I'm ready when they get here, and we can go right away!"

"You don't have to leave right away, silly boy. Your Ma and Liselotte would want to rest for a few days, and maybe we'll celebrate Christmas together."

"No, no, we should go as soon as they get here, we don't have a bed for them and they can't sleep at the plant!"

"Oh, Bram, is that what worries you, that they have to sleep downstairs at the plant? Why don't we ask Oma? Maybe your Mamma and sister could stay with them and sleep in the box bed. Liselotte would like that, wouldn't she?"

"She sure would, Mieneke. She will love it!" he says with a big, happy grin.

School is out for Christmas break. Time seems to slow down and the days drag on for Bram, now that there's nothing else to do but wait.

Opa tries to take him home for a visit, and Peter tells him he's needed at the farm, but he is not leaving the house, in case his mother comes to collect him.

The days before Christmas are dark and grey. The temperature is way below zero.

"We should take Bram on a Christmas tree hunt. That'll keep him occupied for an afternoon," Hank says.

"Just wait a day or so; it's so miserable outside, and maybe it'll warm up soon," Ma says, and she is right.

The weather does get better and, after a light rain during the night, and a mild frost in the early morning hours, the sun comes out, and there's not a cloud in the sky.

I look out the window, and I see the whole world decorated with glistening hoarfrost, wrapped around everything it could find, and sparkles off the trees like long strings of gems, beautifully contrasting against the stark blue sky.

We pull the sled to Peter's house. He quickly dresses warmly and comes along.

"Let's see if Anneke is home; they need a tree too, and maybe she wants to come," Hank says.

It's a gorgeous day for a tree hunt. It's sunny and bright and, with our spirits lifted, we sing all the Christmas carols we know.

"There's a whole row of nice trees right behind your grandparents' home, Mieneke; let's turn into that path and I'll show you where they are." Peter says.

"My Ma would like a tree too, but not too tall," says Anneke.

"And one for our house too," says Peter.

We should have brought another sled!

Bram is in charge of selecting the trees and he's very picky! One tree is too skinny, another one has a hole, yet another one has a flat side and is lopsided. It takes a while, but finally he's satisfied and we load up all the trees.

"One more," Bram says. "That one over there is a perfect little tree for Opa and Oma."

Opa and Oma are home when we drop off their Christmas tree.

"What a nice surprise! The tree is perfect for in here! Did you pick that one, Bram? You're such a good boy! Come in, kids, and I have a surprise for you, too!"

Oma takes a tin of cocoa from the top shelf of the kitchen cupboard.

"I've had this for a long time. I saved it for a special occasion, and today's the perfect day for a nice cup of hot chocolate!"

Bram pulls at my sleeve, puts his mouth close to my ear and whispers: "Can we ask Oma now, Mieneke? Is it okay to ask if Ma and Liselotte can sleep in the box bed?"

Oma looks at him, smiles, and asks Bram to come with her.

"It's all ready for them Bram—come have a look."

He comes back into the kitchen with a happy grin on his face, and says, "It's such a cozy bed for them Mieneke, and Oma knitted a doll for Liselotte and put it on her pillow!"

We drop Anneke and Hank off at the Oostra's house. On the way home, Bram asks Peter if he'll stay to help decorate the tree.

"Mieneke isn't tall enough to put the angel on the top Peter—we need your help!" He looks at me and laughs. It's so good to see him laugh again!

"Are you making fun of me now? You'd better watch out or I'll wash your face with snow!"

"I dare you!" Bram says, and before we know it we're in the middle of a snow-fight!

"Take those wet boots and coats off in the porch," Ma says, "And put yours by the stove to dry, Peter. Leave the tree there to dry before we take it into the front room."

When the tree is decorated, Peter lifts Bram up on his shoulders to put the angel on the top.

"We're finished! Look at that tree! It's the nicest tree we've ever had!"

It's Bram's bedtime, and happily he goes up to the loft. Since Hank is staying over at Anneke's, Bram can sleep in Hank's room, and he loves it!

Peter puts another log on the fire and we snuggle on the sofa. With his arm around my shoulder, and playing with Hanna's ladybug ring, he says, "You should get that ring fixed, Mieneke. Peer's sister makes nice jewelry. She hasn't made anything new lately; she ran out of supplies a while ago, but she does repairs for people, and I know she can make the ring look like new again. Give it to me and I'll ask her tomorrow if you like."

"That would be so nice Peter, I love it!" I run upstairs to get the small ring box. "Don't lose it, please!"

Its seven thirty, and when I walk Peter to the street, we see them.

The woman pushes a handcart with a small child covered with a blanket.

I walk over to her and ask: "Are you Vrouw Boonstra?" And when she nods, I ask her to come inside, and tell her we've been expecting her.

She wears layers of old clothes, and around her worn, thin-soled shoes she wrapped strips of thick cotton. Her fingers, covered with the sleeves of an old sweater, are bent from pushing the cart by the cold metal handle. A long shawl covers her head and face, leaving just a narrow slit for her eyes.

I lift the little girl out of the cart. She's as light as a feather and seems to be very weak.

"Is Bram here? And is he okay?"

"Bram is here—he's sleeping. Let's get you out of these clothes first. Please sit by the fire; you'll need to get warm. We'll get you something to eat first, and then you and your little girl can have a nice warm bath."

Henrika Boonstra, moving almost robotically, lets Ma take over. Liselotte hasn't said a word yet, and when Aunt Jenny removes her shoes she almost falls over.

Ma pulls two chairs close to the fireplace. They sit huddled together when Jenny brings them a tray with a bowl of soup. Henrika tries to spoon-feed her daughter, but the little girl has a hard time swallowing and gags on the chunks of vegetables.

After Pa empties the heavy kettle into the tub, Ma takes mother and daughter into the bathroom.

I'm as quiet as possible, not wanting to wake Bram, when I go upstairs to get a pair of pajamas for the little girl.

I knock on the bathroom door. Liselotte is submerged in the water, and Henrika gently washes her daughter's hair. I quickly hand Ma my pajamas and close the door.

Henrika comes into the kitchen, wearing one of Ma's housecoats, and Liselotte trails right behind her, hiding behind her mother's back. She's so cute with the pajama sleeves and pants rolled up, and her light curly hair still wet. She's the spitting image of her brother, but the poor little girl is so skinny and frail.

Jenny warms up a bowl of soup and purées the vegetables for Liselotte, hoping she'll be able to eat a little bite—but she still can't.

Pa puts some of the bouillon in a cup. "Try to drink this, girl, just a little sip, please, sweetheart—we have to get some nutrients in you."

She looks up and him and, when he smiles, she takes a few sips.

"Good girl," he says, and she smiles at him.

Ma takes Henrika to the front room, and Jenny takes her pillow upstairs. She'll sleep with me tonight.

"You can sleep here, Henrika. It's nice and warm by the fireplace. Maybe we shouldn't wake up Bram; it's better to see him after you have rested, don't you think so?"

"Yes, let him sleep; he needs his strength, too. We'll leave early in the morning."

"Henrika, don't worry about tomorrow. Have a good sleep first; there's no rush."

"I don't want to cause you any more trouble after all you've done for us already. Thank you so much for everything, Anna."

"It's no trouble for us at all. You sleep now, and tomorrow we will see."

"Goodnight—I'll see you in the morning."

Ma slides the doors together, leaving an opening just wide enough to let some of the heat flow into the kitchen.

"Wake up sleepy-head! Wake up, Bram!"

"Why do I have to get up this early? It's not a school day!"

"No, it isn't, but there's somebody downstairs waiting to see you!"

He jumps out bed and runs across the floor. When he gets to the stairs, he turns around. "It's my Ma, isn't it, Mieneke? Is it my Ma and Liselotte?"

And when I smile, he slides down the stair bannister as fast as he can. He runs down the hall to the kitchen, but abruptly stops when he sees his mother.

His arms drop alongside his body, and with tears welling up in his eyes, he says, "Mamma."

She walks up to him, folds him in her arms and says, "Bram, my sweet boy."

And then they cry.

They cry for the loss of his father and his little sister, for all their sorrows and hunger, and for losing their home—but most of all they cry because they can hold each other again.

"You found me, Ma."

"I sure did, my boy, I found you. Let's wake Liselotte now, shall we?"

We all cry when we see the mother and her children huddled together on the mattress in the front room. Ma wipes her eyes with the tip of her apron, and my father turns around so nobody can see him dry his tears with the back of his hand. "Let them be for a while, and I'll make some breakfast," says Ma. "Mieneke, put the kettle on, please."

Liselotte is too weak to get up. Henrika tries to feed her, but after she only swallows a few teaspoons of her porridge, her head falls back in the pillow.

"Let her sleep, Henrika," Ma says. "She needs her rest to get strong again. There's no rush; your child is sick and it's very cold outside. You're not ready to take the trip all the way to Groningen in this weather. Why don't you stay until after Christmas and then we'll see—besides we're used to having Bram around, and would miss that little rascal too much!"

"Can we stay Ma? Can we stay a little longer, please?"

"We will—we'll wait until Liselotte is better!" Henrika answers.

"Yes! Thank you so much Aunt Anna!"

We figure out the sleeping arrangements. Anneke's brother has an extra bed in his room and Hank is welcome to stay there. Jenny takes his bed. Bram can stay on the sofa, and Henrika and Liselotte sleep on the mattress in the front room.

"Problem's solved," Aunty Jenny says.

Anneke and her sisters donate enough clothes for Henrika and her daughter and, with Henrika's permission, we take their old clothes out to the garbage bin.

The following day before I start my route, I talk to the Sister about our visitors. "I will talk to Doctor Veenstra and ask him to come by, and have a look at the little girl," she says, and she does.

That same afternoon the doctor pays them a visit. "They both need good food to get their strength back. The little girl has a nasty lung infection. Keep her warm by the fireplace, but keep the window open just enough to let some fresh air in. Keep an eye on her, and if there's a problem give me a call." He leaves medication for both, and soon after, every day a little more, they seem to get stronger.

On the afternoon of Christmas Eve, we take Henrika to the graveyard. Hank made a simple wooden cross to mark Bas Boonstra's resting place. Henrika, holding Bram's hand, walks over to her husband's grave. With tears in her eyes she wipes the snow of the cross to see his name.

"You can rest now, my love, we're safe. We love you," she says.

Ma takes a candle out of her pocket and hands it, along with a box of matches, to Bram. He lights the candle and, shielding it from the wind with one hand, gives it to his mother, who places it on the grave. After a short little prayer, she takes her son's hand and we follow them home.

Oma, who loves Liselotte, comes over almost every day to bring her little treats. One day she asks Henrika about her relatives in Groningen.

"How well do you know these people, Henrika? Have you ever met them? And do they know you're coming?"

"She's my cousin. I was twelve years old the last time I saw her, and we didn't have regular contact after they moved, but I believe we're welcome—we're family. They live on a big farm outside of the city; there should be enough room."

"Henrika, times are different now, and this war has changed people; would you consider staying here instead?"

"I have no choice Josephine, I have to go. I can't burden your family anymore. All of you have done so much already. I shouldn't outstay my welcome."

"You can stay with us, Henrika. We can clean out the one box bed. Liselotte and you can stay in one, and Bram can sleep in the other. Jochem would love to have you and the kids, and we wouldn't have to worry about you walking all that way with two children. It's so cold, and with the Germans being so miserable and all, will you please think about it?"

And so it happens. The Boonstras move in with Opa and Oma, Hank stays with Anneke, Aunt Jenny sleeps in the loft, and finally we take the mattress out of the front room.

CHAPTER 13

Our liberators come to a standstill when, in September, an airborne assault on Arnhem fails and prevents the liberation of the rest of the Netherlands, but soon we learn that the Canadians have arrived from Italy, and they resume pushing north.

We're hopeful again. We haven't been abandoned! The war will end soon! Our red line on the map crawls up, only millimeters at the time, but it is moving! The Germans know it too, and they seem to get meaner and more vindictive with each passing day.

"Be careful out there," Pa says, "Don't provoke them or get caught by those trigger-happy Nazis!"

February has been the coldest month of this horrible winter so far.

There's a grey drizzly mist all day, and in the late afternoon, the clouds seemingly fall from the sky, and fog lies heavily on the trees. Misty clouds billow over the fields and meadows like smoke from a chimney, and our town is hidden under a blanket of thick fog.

All day I'm somewhat depressed and I can't shake the feeling that something dreadful is about to happen.

"Must be the weather," I can hear my mother say.

Curtains of mist veil themselves around me, making it impossible to see more than four feet ahead of me. I decide that it's probably safer to bike along the edge of the cobblestone road, and stay off the road as much as I can.

Nature built a wall around me, and I feel totally and utterly alone.

As I pass the tennis court's pavilion, I notice every chandelier inside turned on. Through the filtering fog, the light shines on a handful of parked German vehicles and a few bikes. I'm also able to see the silhouettes of a noisy group of soldiers near the vestibule. I hope they can't see me. I cross the road and continue to walk between the ditch and the road.

I hear a vehicle, but when I look back, I can't see it. Like an animal on the prowl, the throaty sound of the engine comes closer and I move toward the ditch. When I look back again, the headlights, like a predator's yellow eyes, emerge from the fog. I stop and wish I could shrink myself, so as not to been seen by the driver. I'm hoping the vehicle keeps going on its way.

It passes me, at a slower pace than circumstances would allow, as if searching, but luckily the headlights don't have a wide enough range to see me, or so I think.

When I see the red rear lights through the mist, I breathe a sigh of relief and step back toward the road.

The sound of the engine suddenly changes, and now I see the red lights coming toward me. It frightens me, but there isn't enough time to hide.

The car stops beside me, and when he rolls down the window I see his scarred, smirking face.

"Well, well, and who do we have here? If it isn't the little nurse. It's Mieneke, isn't it?"

He opens the car door and steps out.

"It's nasty out here and not safe for a young girl. Can I give you a lift?"

In one hand he holds a riding whip and slaps it, rhythmic almost, into his other leather gloved hand.

"No, thank you Werner, I'm almost home."

I push my bike, and after running a few meters, jump on and pedal as fast as I can, but not fast enough!

Through the fog, I can hear the snap of the whip, and the leather rope twists itself around the spokes and brings me to an abrupt halt.

Scarcheek hauls me in, like a fisherman reeling in his catch.

"What's you hurry, sweet girl? Are you in a rush to get to your little Dutch boyfriend? Come sit in the car and we'll have a drink. I've asked you before, but you always said no, and here you are again. It must be destiny that I have you all to myself now!"

"I have to get home. My parents will be worried and will look for me if I'm not home on time. Another day maybe?"

Scarcheek laughs and says, "Stop treating me like a fool, Mieneke. Now let's have a drink." He hands me a flask.

"I don't drink Werner. Please let me go home."

"Why are you in such a rush, uh? You want to meet up with your boyfriend? Why waste your time on a boy when you can have a real man, eh Mieneke? I've been watching you, and every time I see you with that boy you piss me off! So drink!"

He slaps my rain hat to the ground, grabs my hair and twists it around his hand. He puts the flask to my lips, but I close my mouth and turn my face away.

"You nasty bitch, look what you've done! You've made me spill it all!"

He pulls my head back, grabs my chin, and when I turn away again, he tightens his grip around my jaw and roughly kisses me on my lips. I can smell the alcohol on his breath. I resist and jerk my head to the side.

"Let me go Werner! You have Coba!"

He laughs again.

"Coba? Coba is just a little whore! No, I want you! I wanted you all along and I know you want me too. I saw that horny look in your eyes every time we met. You know I can do things to you that your shitty little boyfriend would never do to you! I'll make you feel like a woman—a real woman, Mieneke!"

"Let me go!"

"Let you go? Let you go to your boy? Oh no, my liebling! I have to show you first what it's like to get it from a real man!"

I try to pull away from him, but his hand comes down hard across my face. An intense pain shoots through my nose and up between my eyes. My teeth cut through my bottom lip. I can't breathe! The metallic, bloody taste in my throat makes me gag, and I almost pass out. I spit out the blood and ask him again to please let me go, but he sneers and jerks my head back again. "Not before you tell me you want me. Say it, say it, you little whore! Say it, 'I want you Werner, I want it!' *Say it!*"

"No! Let me go!"

He tries to kiss me again, but when he forces his tongue into my mouth, I bite his lip.

"Goddamned filthy bitch!" he yells.

I'm able to pull free and try to get away again, but he grabs my arm, and with one quick move turns me around. I can feel the bone snap like a dry twig and like a bolt of lightning, an excruciating pain cuts through my arm. He smashes my face on the trunk of the car and holds me down. With his other hand he throws my coat over my head and violently rips down my pants. I struggle, but he's too strong. His knees pin me down against the car. His hands reach under my sweater and he grabs my breast, and pinches my nipples so hard that it makes me scream out in pain.

"Shut up bitch, one more sound and you're dead!"

He takes the belt from my coat and ties it tight around my broken wrist. It makes me scream again. The handle of the whip hits me across my back. His hands dig into my bare bottom and spreads my buttock with such force, that it feels as if he's ripping my lower body in two.

"Never had it from behind, did you liebchen? Your Dutch boy never did this to you, did he, did he? Answer me!"

He bends over, and I can feel the heat of his words hiss in my ear.

"You like it, yes? Say you like it. Say it! Say it!"

All I do is pray. *Please God send me somebody to save me from this beast, please, before he kills me!*

I can feel his hard, hot member against my naked lower back. I struggle again. That son of a bitch is going to rape me, and I'm fighting for my life! He hits me with a closed fist across the back of my head, almost knocking me out. With one arm he pulls my lower body against his abdomen and with his other hand he holds me down. He's going to rape me and then he's going to kill me! I have no fight left in me.

"You're a coward! Go ahead, coward, and do it bastard!"

He smacks me again, but I don't care anymore, I've lost the fight.

He grabs my buttocks again, and I know that this is it, I'm going to die and I pray.

I hear a dull thud like a bat hitting a baseball, and his body goes limp. He lays sprawled over my back, nearly suffocating me. I can't move and I can't breathe! Somebody's strong hands roll him off me. I gasp and when I try to swallow, I start coughing up blood.

"Here now, let me help you, don't worry, you're safe."

The friendly voice sounds familiar, and through my swollen eyes, I recognize the tall soldier I saw at Vrouw Oost' house. He pulls up my pants and straightens out my coat. He then lifts me off the car and gently puts me in the front seat.

After he unties my wrists, he takes a clean handkerchief from his pocket and holds it against my bleeding nose. "Hold it there and put some pressure on it."

I must have looked so frightened, because he says: "Don't be scared, child, I'll take you home. You're safe now."

Werner Scarcheek lays unconscious beside the car with his face in a muddy puddle. The soldier hides his bike in the ditch and then pulls Zimmerman through the ditch and, using Zimmerman's own belt, ties him to a tree. He puts my bike in the trunk and covers me with his jacket before he takes the driver's seat.

"My name is Hans Merkel," he says. "I will take you home, and then I'll take Zimmerman to the office and lock him up for the night. I will make sure he gets punished for what he did to you. I promise you, he will not get away with this. My poor child, I'm so sorry!"

We drive home through the fog without saying another word.

He carries me to the house and knocks. My mother opens the door.

"Dear God, Mieneke, what in the world happened to you?"

She looks at Merkel. "What happened? Who did this?" she demands.

"Not now. I'm sorry, but you have to take care of your daughter. I have to go back and take that criminal to the office and lock him up till Kaiser comes back tomorrow. I'll be back in the morning to see how she's doing. I will report this horrible abuse to Kaiser, he'll deal with him and he won't be kind. Tell your husband to come to the office in the morning, please. I'll make sure Kaiser is expecting him."

He puts me down in Pa's chair and quickly leaves the kitchen.

Ma takes me to her bedroom where she carefully takes off my clothes and wraps me in her housecoat. Jenny already put hot water in the tub, and Ma supports me when I lower myself in the bath.

"I'll be back in a sec sweetheart," Ma says. She comes back with a bottle of Minnie's lotion and empties the entire bottle into my bathwater.

"Jenny, please phone the doctor and Martin."

I can't talk, not yet, and Ma doesn't ask any questions. All I do is sob. Ma gently washes my face and hair. She carefully sponges my body with a soft cloth, all the while talking to me as if I were an infant.

She rolls up a towel and puts it under my arm to take the weight off my broken wrist. "I think the doctor is here. I'll let him in. Are you okay for a few seconds?"

I lay in the tub and I sob.

I must have said something stupid again, like I did that time when he asked us to come for Christmas dinner. *Oh Hanna, I didn't have your ladybug ring or I would have been okay! What did I say? It must have been something nasty. Did I open my big mouth again?* I go over it and over it again in my head. Anneke was right.

I must have provoked him! I can't keep my big mouth shut! It's my own fault! I should have let him take me home, and that would have been the end of it. This would not have happened. It's my own fault!

Ma comes in and helps me out of the tub. She dries me with the fluffiest towel she could find and takes me to her bedroom, where the doctor examines me.

"Your nose is badly bruised, but not broken. You do have a fractured wrist, a few cuts, and those bruises are nasty and will hurt for a while," he says.

"How did this happen, Mieneke who did this to you? Can you tell me?"

"It was a German soldier. His name is Zimmerman, Werner Zimmerman. Uh...I...I must have said something stupid, and it made him mad. He lost his temper...I was an idiot, it's my own fault."

"I don't believe that for a minute. Something like this can't be your fault, but we'll talk later. You'll get some rest now. I'll give you something for the pain and a sleeping pill, and tomorrow morning I'll be back and set your wrist. Try to sleep now, okay?"

Ma brings me a glass of water and the pills. She puts the glass to my cut lips; it hurts to swallow, but I manage to get the pills down. Ma tells me to get into her bed and tucks me in before she sees the doctor out.

I can hear my father's voice in the kitchen. He opens the door and peeks inside.

"Can I come in Mieneke? My dear girl! Sweetheart, I'm so sorry!"

"Papa," is all I can say, and when he puts his arms around me I cry.

I feel drowsy, my body is heavy, my broken wrist throbs, and I can barely breathe through my bruised, swollen nose. I close my eyes, and somewhere in the distance, I can hear the bedroom door close. I pass out into a deep empty sleep.

I wake up and find Ma beside me. I'm confused. Why am I in my parent's bed? When I turn over and feel the pain, I remember.

Ma stirs and turns toward me.

"Mieneke, you're awake. How did you sleep? Are you in a lot of pain? Can I get you something? Do you want another pill? Doctor Veenstra left a few, just in case."

"Ma, I could have slept in my own bed. Where is Papa? What time is it?"

"It's still early, twenty past five. Pa is sleeping in your bed. Can I get you something to drink? Do you have to go to the bathroom? Can you get up? Here sweetheart, let me help you."

I'm still drowsy and it does hurt to move, but with Ma's help, I make it to the bathroom.

"I'm okay now, Ma."

"I'll make breakfast. What would you like? Coffee or tea? Do you want it in bed?"

"It doesn't matter what you make, Ma, and I'll come to the kitchen."

"Please, don't lock the door, Mieneke, just in case."

I look in the mirror, and the face I see is that of a stranger and it shocks me. My swollen nose makes my eyes stand wide apart and my lip is cut and bruised. I hardly recognize myself. I open the bathrobe and see the bruises on my breasts. His black and blue fingerprints, as if I'm marked there forever, make me shudder, and I quickly close the robe. I lower myself carefully on the toilet. It hurts to sit down. I get frustrated when I try to pull up my panties, and I start to cry, hoping Ma can't hear me.

Now I'm getting mad. *That son of a bitch! I won't let him get away with this, he'll pay! I don't know how yet, but he will pay for this!* I wipe my tears and slowly walk to the kitchen.

"Try to eat something; you must be hungry—you didn't have dinner last night."

My mother is fussing and worried about me, I know, but I'm not hungry. I nibble on the bread just to please her. I'm not looking forward to my father coming downstairs. I know they'll ask me questions, and I don't know what to say. I'm too embarrassed and ashamed. How can I tell them what Scarcheek did to me? Especially my father, I won't be able to tell him the details and, oh my God, Peter! I have to face Peter too! He'll be disgusted, and mad too for letting Scarcheek do this to me. How can I explain this to him?

My father comes downstairs and sits down beside me. He takes my hand and says: "I know you're hurting sweetheart, and it'll take some time to get better. We will get the guy who did this to you, I swear. I talked to the doctor last night, and he'll be by this morning to set your wrist. I told him to make a report and we'll take it to Kaiser. I don't care who this bastard thinks he is, but he will be punished. He told me it's not going to be easy for you to talk about it, but please tell Doctor Veenstra exactly what that Nazi did to you, he needs to know, okay sweetheart?"

"Mieneke, did that soldier rape you? Sorry to ask you, but I need to know," Ma asks, after my father leaves the room.

"He...he...was going to, but then that other soldier came and...he stopped him." I put my face in my hand. *My God, this is so awkward. I can't talk about it!*

"It's alright, sweetheart; that's all I need to know. We can talk about it later when you're ready."

There's a knock on the door and Doctor Veenstra and Sister Kamp walk in.

"How are you, Mieneke?" He examines my nose. "Oh, there is a small fracture, but it should heal properly; your nose is still straight. I will set your wrist. It'll hurt, but I'll give you another pain killer, and you can have another pill to help you sleep later." He sets my wrist between two splints and tightly winds a bandage around it. "Please, turn on your stomach Mieneke. I like to have another look at those bruises on your back and the bump on your head. Can you tell me what happened yesterday and what he did to you?"

"I...I..." I stammer.

"Would you rather have Sister Kamp talk to you about it? It's okay if you do, I understand. Here is a soothing salve for the bruises; you have to take it easy for a while. Do you feel dizzy? Do you feel like throwing up?" he asks when looking in my eyes.

"No, no—I'm just tired and sore."

"Good, you don't have a concussion, but take your time to get better, Mieneke; there's no rush."

We go back to the kitchen, and before the doctor leaves, he tells Pa he'll come to the plant at eleven thirty and they will go to Kaiser.

"Please write a report, Sister, so we can take it to the German's office. Mieneke, if you need anything, you'll let the sister know. I'll come by in a few days to see how you are."

"It's hard to talk about what Scarcheek did, but Sister Kamp is so kind and understanding. She doesn't mind when I cry, and tells me to take my time. After I tell her everything, as well as I can, she tells me to rest.

"Take another pill, Mieneke, and try to sleep. This is enough for now, but we will talk again. You have to talk to somebody in order to deal with it. It'll take some time, but I'm always here for you. You have a good family; they'll support you, and after a while you'll be fine, I promise."

I tell Ma I can go upstairs, but she has none of it.

"No Mieneke, you'll stay down here—you're closer to the bathroom, and I can keep an eye on you."

Hanna is in my dream.

We're walking in the field behind van Holt's farm. We're picking flowers—flowers for Oma. I carry one of Opa's rabbits in a basket. The rabbit is big and heavy.

"Help me carry the basket, Hanna. It's so heavy, and carrying it by myself hurts my wrist." We hear somebody walking behind us, trying to catch up.

We hear his heavy breathing. We look back and see a soldier. He doesn't have a face—or maybe we can't see his face?

"Give me the rabbit!" he shouts. "Give it to me! You can't have it! You're stealing food from the army! You're thieves! Say it, say it! I'm a thief! Say it! I want it, give it to me!"

Hanna starts to scream. "No, let us go! I have to go to my Ma and Pa. Davie! Where are you? Wait for me!"

"Hanna, Hanna!"

Ma is here. She wipes my hot feverish face with a cool damp cloth.

"Mieneke, hush, my sweetheart, it's just a bad dream. You're at home, you're safe."

"Oh Mamma," I say, and then I cry for a long time. When there are no tears left, I tell her everything, and she cries too.

"I was so scared Mamma. I fought and fought, but had no strength left after a while. He was so strong! I was sure he was going to kill me and all I could think of was all of you, and I thought that now for sure, I would never see Hanna again!"

Ma puts her arms around me, and she rocks me back and forth like she did when I was a baby.

"Hans Merkel was here to see how you are. He told me he saw somebody pass the pavilion where they had a meeting, and shortly after he noticed Zimmerman had left without him. Knowing Zimmerman, he knew something was wrong. He took somebody's bike and followed Zimmerman. When he saw what was going on, he sneaked up from behind and knocked Zimmerman over the head with his pistol. Thank God he did."

"He brought a basket with fruit. He's such a decent man. I feel sorry for him; he doesn't want this war, he just wants to go home and be with his family again. Poor man! Damn Hitler!"

It's already two thirty when Pa and the doctor return from the German office. "He's dead. Zimmerman was shot early this morning," Pa says.

"Kaiser must have executed him himself."

They sit down, and after Ma pours them each a coffee, they tell us what happened at the office.

"My apologies are not enough to tell you how sorry I am for what happened to your daughter. Zimmerman was a fanatic criminal, and there were too many incidents before this one," Kaiser said. "This time he went too far. I know many atrocities have happened during this war. I don't like it, but there's nothing I can do about it. I have to follow orders. However, I cannot and will not tolerate the rape and torture of an innocent girl, not under my watch! Zimmerman was a sadist, a rapist and a coward, who liked to prey on the weak and vulnerable. He wasn't a soldier! I couldn't deal with his crimes anymore. That is why, this time, I had to take the law into my own hands. Please follow me," Kaiser said.

"He took us to a room in the back and showed us Zimmerman's body. When we walked through the hall back to his office, he turned to me and asked me that, if I had to write a report, could I write that it was suicide? And could we please keep it confidential?" Doctor Veenstra says.

"He a strange man, a strange man indeed; I don't know if I hate him or feel sorry for him. I'd better be on my way. I have a few more patients to see. Call me if you need me. Thanks for the coffee Anna."

"The doctor is right—he is a strange fellow, that Kaiser," Pa says.

"He asked me if he could shake my hand, and said again how bad he feels for what Zimmerman did, and then he asked me if he could do anything for Mieneke. I told him, 'No. We will manage.'"

It feels strange. Zimmerman is dead and his death weighs heavy on me. *Did I cause his death? Am I responsible? Did he have a wife and children?*

When Sister Kamp comes for a visit later that afternoon, we have a long talk.

"I know it will take a while before you'll come to terms with this Mieneke, but remember, it was Zimmerman himself who caused his death. It had nothing to do with you. You're the victim who just happened to be there, at the wrong place and at the wrong time. Let it go and get better, and take your time. I'm always available if you need to talk."

Peter comes by the following day. I don't know if I can face him, but Ma invites him in and she comes into the bedroom to get me.

"You do have to talk to him, Mieneke. He loves you and he's worried—please talk to him."

Peter is in the front room. His back is turned to me when I walk in.

"Peter?"

He turns around, and I cover my face in my hands before he can have a good look at me.

"My darling, it's alright, it's me," and he gently removes my hands and softy kisses my sore bruised lips.

"It's alright, sweetheart, we'll be fine," he says, and wraps me in his strong arms.

Margie and I are on the patio soaking up the early spring sun when a German truck pulls into the driveway. It frightens me, and I jump up to run into house, but when I see a tall man crawl out of the back, I stop.

He's skin and bones and his clothes hang off his thin skeleton-like body. He looks familiar, and when he walks up to us, I recognize Uncle Jan.

"Mieneke," he says.

"Oh my God, it's you, Uncle Jan!"

Before I can hug him, Aunt Jenny comes running out of the house.

"Jan, Jan! You're home!"

90

He reaches out to her and takes her in his arms. They stand there for a long time, crying and laughing, until Ma takes them inside.

"Mieneke, run to the plant and get your father and Hank!"

"Go inside with them, Mieneke, and I'll tell your father before I go home," says Margie.

"I didn't believe anymore that I would ever see any of you again," Uncle Jan says. "And when they came into our quarters, at four o'clock in the morning, I thought my time was up. I had seen so many go before me, never to return, and I thought this time it was me who was to be hanged or shot. I was shocked when they took me to a room where they deloused me, and I was told I was going home! They didn't tell me why I was the lucky one, and I didn't ask any questions. They gave me a lump of bread for on the way. Three times they put me in a different truck, and I was told to hide under a pile of sacks when we went through the check points. It was as if we were on a secret mission. Once and a while they threw some food at me; it was more than I ever had in the prison so I didn't complain. It wouldn't have done me any good anyways, because they could still kill me, and that's all I could think about. I didn't really believe I was going home, until I peeked through a slit in the tarp and saw the sign of our town. I can't believe it! I'm home and I survived! Praise the Lord, but why me?"

And that's all he tells us. He doesn't talk about his cell mates, the conditions in the prison, nothing, not to us, but I know he talks to my father.

We put the mattress back in the front room.

We all believe Kaiser has something to do with my uncle's sudden release, and if that's the case, then I'm thankful something good came out of this, and it makes me feel a lot better. I still have bad dreams and nasty flashbacks from that horrible ordeal, and sometimes I have a hard time going outside by myself on a foggy day, but everybody is so kind and understanding, and every day I feel a little stronger.

CHAPTER 14

It's my birthday. I think of Hanna, and wonder if she celebrated her birthday. I never received another letter, and I never did find anybody to return a letter to her. I don't know if she's still with the same people in Friesland. I think about her every day, and worry about her all the time. Will I ever see her again? Will she and her family come home? We've heard stories about the camps where the Jews and other "undesirables" were imprisoned and from the few things we heard from Uncle Jan, we know those prisons are horrible. Was Hanna caught and sent to one of those camps, and were her parents brought there too? Where are they? My birthdays have never been the same since Hanna left. I remember the happy birthdays we celebrated with our families. I remember Minnie's kugels and latkes and her beautiful braided breads. I remember Davie, playing the piano and all of us singing "Happy Birthday." It seems so long ago, I miss it and most of all I miss Hanna so much!

I don't feel like celebrating my birthday and I ask my mother not to make a big fuss. I'm not in the mood.

Peter comes over in the afternoon and stays for supper. We're in the backyard when he puts his arms around me.

"Happy birthday, sweetheart," he says, and hands me a small box.

"Peter, you shouldn't have bought a birthday gift!"

"I didn't, and it isn't really yours, but I know you'll like it, so come on, open it!"

I open the present and recognize the small silver jewelry box. Hanna's ladybug ring is, except for a few tiny little scratches, as good as new!

"Oh Peter, that's the best present ever! Thank you, thank you so much!"

He puts the ring on the thin silver chain and clasps it around my neck. "Now you can return it to Hanna when she comes home."

"The war will be over soon, Mieneke. The Queen visited the liberated provinces. I read it in the paper. She was back in the Netherlands!"

"We're on the Threshold of Freedom," one of the headlines said."

When we hear rumors about the Canadians coming closer, Peter and I spread our map on the floor and continue our red line.

The Germans are dangerous. They do anything to stay ahead of their allied enemies, and often act irrational and unpredictable.

"They're like animals backed into a corner. Stay away from them if you can, they're dangerous," Pa warns us.

We see small groups of soldiers march through our town. They're old men and boys as young as twelve years old. They look pitiful in their ill-fitting uniforms and boots, not at all like the proud confident troops that marched through our town five years ago.

We notice more soldiers from the city here too, making our lives as miserable as they can. They steal our bikes, chickens, rabbits and whatever else they think they have the right to confiscate. They seem desperate and hungry.

"The worm has turned," my mother says.

Anneke comes over and is still shaking when she tells us of the ordeal they went through at her home.

Three soldiers stormed into their house earlier this morning. They were looking for her brother, Hilbert. When Anneke's father told them he had no idea where to find his son, one of the soldiers—"Just a teenager," Anneke says—pointed his pistol at her father's chest.

"Where is your son?" he said, and when her father told him again that he didn't know, the boy hit him with the butt of his revolver across the face, knocking out two of her father's teeth. Three more times, he was asked the same question and three more times he was hit across his face.

Hilbert in the meantime, was hiding in the narrow space above the sliding doors. "Similar to the sliding doors here," Anneke says.

They removed a few planks in the attic, and that gave him enough room to slide into the pocket above the doors. They covered the loose planks with a mattress, complete with bedding and pillows, hoping the soldiers would miss the hiding place if they ever came by.

The Germans searched the whole house. First they emptied the kitchen cupboards—"As if we would hide him in there," she says.

Pots and pans, broken cups and dishes were scattered all over the floor. Then they went through the bedrooms.

Anneke's sister, who's pregnant, had a box with baby clothes stored on the top shelf above her bed.

"Ah, that's must be the radio!" one of the Germans said and stepped on the bed. He reached for the box and, expecting it to be heavy, braced himself to take it down. The unexpected light weight of the contents threw him off and, losing his footing, he tumbled backwards over the bed and landed on the floor, covered under baby clothes.

"When I think about it now, I realize how funny it was, but at the time we didn't laugh, we were too scared," she says.

The soldier lost his temper and pointing his gun to the ceiling, he systematically, in rows across the entire ceiling, "Rat-a-tat-tat," emptied his gun's chamber. Nobody dared to look up to the top of the sliding doors, scared to give away the hiding place, but they're almost sure Hilbert must've been hit by a bullet. Dust and chunks of plaster fell down from the ceiling, covering everything—including the soldiers, who, totally ticked off by now, finally leave, but not before they shout a few more threats and warnings.

"The house is a mess, but miraculously Hilbert is alive. One of the bullets missed him by only half of a centimeter. My God, this war has to end before they shoot us all!" Anneke says.

CHAPTER 15

A few days after my birthday, on April 10, the French paratroopers land in a farmer's field near our town. They're here! Soon the war will be over!

The French immediately contact our resistance team, who assist the paratroopers with securing the bridges, and supply guides for the approaching Canadians.

In the excitement, people already start celebrating the assumed victory over the Germans. A dangerous situation arises when some of the young men take the law in their own hands and severely beat up a few of the local N.S.B. members. One of the beaten up men escapes to the city and reports the unrest to his son, who works closely with the German SS.

Cor Dekker is worried about the nasty incident that happened in town and asks Pa if he can borrow his bike. He wants to ask the French, who are hiding with a family across the field, to assist with the arrest of all the local collaborators, and to hopefully avoid similar confrontations.

Everybody is worried the Germans will retaliate and come to town to do some serious damage, and most people stay inside, fearing the worst.

It's one o'clock in the afternoon when two covered army trucks speed into town. Soldiers jump out the back and immediately divide into two groups. One group seems to be on their way to confront the paratroopers, and the other group spreads out and, at random, starts to arrest men around town.

My father is getting worried about Cor Dekker, who hasn't returned yet, and who must be unaware of what's happening in town. He doesn't know of the arrival of the Germans or what they're up to, and might very well fall into the hands of our occupiers on his way back to town. Pa talks to Paul de Wal, and they decide to look for Cor to warn him before he runs into the Germans.

Eleven men and boys, between the age of fourteen and sixty two, have been arrested. The Germans line them up against the forest wall by the graveyard. They stand with their hands above their heads for hours, not knowing their fate. Among them is Tom Tiemen, who just happened to be outside to take out the garbage when he was arrested.

The streets are empty, when at eight o'clock in the evening a German jeep, with tires squealing, comes around the corner and stops in front of the captured men. The irate SS commander, furiously ranting and raving, jumps out of the vehicle. He grabs his automatic weapon and without any thought or warning, empties his gun on the innocent men. They all perish, except Tom, who miraculously, and although slightly hurt, lies under the dead bodies for hours until, when he thinks it's safe to move, he manages to flee without being seen.

The people can hear the gun shots and the screams, and when the sounds stop and it turns eerily quiet outside, they know. The next morning they find the bodies of the murdered men, and everybody is devastated.

The townspeople collect the bodies and take them to the old gym where Sister Kamp and the ladies from the Red Cross take care of the dead men. They place them on biers, and the people look through the row to find their loved ones.

The anticipation and excitement of being liberated has vanished. How long yet, and what else will happen before the Nazis are defeated and we will be free again? We're all afraid the Nazis will return and cause more destruction.

My father didn't come home. We can hear the sounds of gun battle and see black clouds near the field where the Paratroopers landed. There must be a fire. We know there's heavy fighting, and we pray Pa and the other men are in a safe place, and that the French will defeat the Germans. Can they hold on until more allied troops arrive? How many French are fighting the Germans? Will the Nazis send reinforcements?

We are sick with worry and stay inside, afraid to go outside and get caught in the fight in case it spreads out into the town.

A knock on the door makes us jump, and Ma carefully opens the door to see who's there. When she opens the door wider, she sees the oldest daughter of Frederik Wolters.

"Come in, come in and sit down," she says, thinking the girl is looking for shelter.

"No, I just came to give you a message from my father. I want to go home right away, in case the fighting comes this way. I come to tell you that Martin won't come home tonight. My father gave him a ride in his wagon when he came off the field. Martin is hiding in the woods, that's all my father knows. I'd better go now."

We're thankful the young woman took the risk and brought us the message, but we're still very worried, and don't go to bed that night. We sit at the table and try to concentrate on playing a game of cards, but we're preoccupied with worries. Where is my father? Will the Germans come back? What in the world will happen next?

The Canadians force their troops across the border of our province and liberate the cities and towns south of us.

In the afternoon of April 11, they occupy the town across the canal, and although the Canadian commander has been informed and is aware of the situation in our town, he is unable to move forward. He's waiting for materials to fix the bridge, but the shipment might take another three days to arrive. They're stuck on the other side of the canal. Uncle Jan, worried about the return of the Germans, gets a group of volunteers together, and they gather materials from the other bridges. During the night, under supervision of the Canadian commander and Uncle Jan's boss, they build a temporary bridge. Early in the morning the Canadians cross the bridge and enter our town.

My father comes home in the afternoon. He was shot, but other than a flesh wound underneath his left ear, he's okay. After he rests for a few hours, he tells us of his ordeal:

"We knew the Paratroopers were hiding across the meadow, where they had landed on April 10, but how many there were exactly we didn't know. We knew they were there, because a few people reported to us that they had seen them. Cor had seen them too, and that's why he asked to borrow my bike—to find the paratroopers and ask for help after what happened in town.

"We were worried about him when the Germans suddenly appeared in town, and decided to see if we could find him. We were hoping to intercept him when he came out of the woods and crossed the field, which we believed he would do. When we were ready to move ahead, we came face-to-face with two German soldiers, and we had no other choice than to run! That's when the firing started, and Paul and I were smack in the middle of the firing line. Germans were shooting on one side at whatever moved in the woods, and the French fired back from across the meadow. We ran for our lives, trying to make it across the field and over the forest wall on the other side. Paul, who's a lot heavier than I, couldn't run as fast, and was a few meters behind me. I looked back and yelled at him to go faster! Before we reached the wall the bullets were whistling around us, and I started zigzagging through the field, hoping Paul would follow my lead. I looked back again and saw Paul sprawled out in the grass. It didn't make any sense to me that he would lay down right there! I yelled at him to get up! I didn't realize he was hit! I felt a sharp pain on the side of my head, but kept running, unaware I was hit too!

"I lost my wooden shoes and, in my stocking feet, I reached the top of the wall and was out of the Germans sight. Panicked, I kept running until suddenly I realized that I might run into another dangerous situation! The paratroopers! How would they know I wasn't the enemy?

"My first instinct was to hide in the ditch and stay there until the fighting was over, but then I saw Frederik Wolters, who, strangely enough, seemed unaware of the dangerous and dire situation, and was returning home from his field with his horse and wagon. He had suddenly appeared, and I didn't know what else to do than to jump into the back of his wagon. We only spoke a few words, but Frederik seemed to be aware of the perilous situation I was in. After I only rode with him for a few hundred meters, I jumped off the wagon and ran back into the woods. I'm very thankful he sent his daughter to tell you that I was alive. I wandered through the dense woods for a while, hoping to avoid the paratroopers until, after a few hours, I came to the farm of Bertus de Vries, whom I know; they took me in. Vrouw de Vries looked after my wound as good as she could. It was there that I met the first paratroopers, who told me how dangerous the situation in our town was, and advised me to stay put until it was safe to leave. After two days I left, and when I walked into town I saw our Canadian liberators. Thank God the war is over!

"Before I came home, I stopped at the Red Cross building where Sister Kamp looked after my head wound, and she told me of the sad fate of the captured men, and that my dear friend Paul hadn't made it and had died right there in the meadow.

"This certainly was the most frightening, saddest and happiest day of my life," my father says.

CHAPTER 16

Dutch flags, ribbons and flowers appear out of nowhere. The streets are a sea of orange, red, white and blue with waves of ecstatic people, who sing and dance through downtown. The Dutch flag hangs out of nearly every window, from the roofs of buildings and the church tower. People play the Dutch anthem on their harmonicas and music echoes through the streets. We dance to the music of the carillon that's playing on the street corner again. We wave orange streamers, and young women and girls jump on the Canadian vehicles to kiss their heroes and cover them with colorful tulips.

All the N.S.B. and Youth Storm members, together with other collaborators, are arrested by the resistance team and put in temporary holding cells. The Germans are rounded up, disarmed and guarded by Canadian soldiers in a field behind the hotel.

Peter and I are among the celebrators and we're swept along by the crowd of singing and dancing youngsters. Young men put the Canadian soldiers on their shoulders and carry them high above the people. We can't get enough of the crazy high we're on.

The Canadians hand out Players Light cigarettes, and throw candies, gum and chocolates from the vehicles and I see Bram among the children, his pockets bulging with sweets.

We make our way through a noisy group of people gathered in the town square to see what all the excitement is about.

A few young women are surrounded by the jeering crowd. Coba Mos, who's clearly pregnant, is one of the women.

"Nazi whores, Nazi whores!" the people jeer. "Shave them and tar them, shave them bald!"

Egged on by the crowd, they're placed on a farmer's wagon and, for all to see, somebody proceeds to shave off their hair with a set of barber clippers. Another person is waiting with a can of paint, and when the shaving is done, he paints the bald head with bright orange paint. They're pulled up, ordered to raise their arms and yell, as loud as they can: "Long live the Queen, long live the Queen!"

"Louder, louder!" the crowd roars.

"Long live the Queen!"

Coba's eyes meet mine. Her stare is so cold and full of hate that it sends a shiver down my spine. Does she know what happened to Werner Zimmerman, how and why he died, and that it had something to do with me?

The whole nasty scene is sickening and turns my stomach. I push through the crowd, thinking I can make it stop, but Peter pulls me back.

"Let it be Mieneke, let it go, and let's get out of here."

Coba is lowered from the wagon and her brother throws his jacket over her head, but in one movement she throws it back at him and, with her head held high and a proud look in her eyes, she makes her way through the crowd and walks away.

We meet up with our friends at the hotel. Somebody has opened the café and we all get a beer. The German propaganda is pulled down from the façade, is thrown in the street and is now covered with mud and dirty footprints. Hitler's portrait has been torn down, too. Somebody cut it in long strips, painted it orange, attached it to a long pole, and it's now flapping in the breeze out of the hotel's window. A harmonica man plays all the Dutch songs, and we sing and dance to his music till the early morning hours.

Our town, our country and our people are free again. The war is over!

Great is the contrast between the celebrators and the ones who mourn their loved ones. It will be a long time before our lives will be back to what it was before the war—if it ever will be the same again.

CHAPTER 17

Hanna should be coming home soon, and I feel we should get everything ready for her and her family's arrival.

Father changes the lock of the back door, and Margie and I clean the Bloch's house. We wash and paint the walls. Father removes the broken furniture and the paint stained mattress. Peter managed to get his hands on a French parachute and Aunt Jenny uses it to sew new curtains for every window. We go around town for donations and collect pots and pans, furniture, mattresses and bedding. After a week of cleaning and decorating the house, although not as fancy as it used to be, it is cozy and livable again.

Ma and I are on our way to my grandparent's house when we see the retreating German troops, and we join other people on the street corner to see them leave town.

There are no proud officers shouting orders, no fancy cars or tanks. What we see is a defeated army, unarmed, unshaven and with torn dirty uniforms, walking out of town, like a dog with the tail between his legs.

"Go home, dirty Nazis! Go home!" a man yells and throws a stone at one of the officers, but nobody else joins him. The people on the street quietly watch as the prisoners, flanked by their Canadian captors, walk by.

I see Hans Merkel, and when he sees me too, he gives me a quick nod and a brief smile. I smile at him, and I know we're both glad that he goes home to be with his family again.

Bram sits at the table when we walk into Oma's kitchen. He looks sick!

"What's wrong Bram? Your cheeks are swollen—are you okay?"

"He's fine. Henrika took him to the doctor this morning. We thought he had the mumps, but he chewed gum all day yesterday and that's what made his jaws swell like a little hamster's, isn't that right, Bram?" Oma said and ruffled his hair.

"Oh, Bram," I say and hug him, trying not to laugh!

"No more sweets—only one a day for a while, that's the deal, eh, Bram?"

"I know, Oma, I know."

"Is Opa home?"

"He's outside in the back, I believe."

Opa sits on the bench by the holly hedge, smoking his pipe. I sit beside him and, after we talk for a while, we hear somebody move about behind the hedge. Opa, quietly, goes around the rabbit cages and peeks around the corner.

"Hey there," Opa yells, and a young soldier stops in his tracks. He turns around and, clearly frightened, he looks at us and then starts to cry. Dark wet lines run down his cheeks. The poor child is maybe twelve years old, dirty, and in a uniform way too big for him. He looks so scared.

"What's your name son?" Opa asks.

"Klaus...Klaus Berger."

"And what are you doing here, Klaus?"

"I ran away. I can't walk anymore, my feet are so sore. Where do we go, where are they taking us? I'm so hungry. I don't have a home or Fatherland anymore—all is lost," he says in German.

Opa tells him to sit down on the bench and take off his boots. We can't believe our eyes when we see the poor boy's feet. His toes are cramped from walking in boots way too small for him, and his dirty socks rub into his open and bleeding blisters.

We take him into the kitchen and Oma gets him a plate of leftovers.

"Eat, Klaus," Opa says. "Where are you from, where are your parents?"

"Bielefeld, but my parents, I don't know. Maybe they're dead? Bombs, bombs," he says, and with his arms he imitates the falling of bombs.

"We can't send him away now, Jochem," Oma says.

"But Josephine, we have to!"

"No Jochem, he's just a child; we'll keep him here until all this excitement has settled down and that's it!"

"Bielefeld is not far from here and we can find out, through the Red Cross, where his parents live," my mother says.

Ma finds civilian clothes for him, and he learns to walk in wooden shoes. Opa burns his German uniform and worn-out boots in a barrel in the backyard.

We do find out, with the help of the Red Cross, that his parents are alive and well in Bielefeld, and Pa and Hank drive him to the border and hand him to the Canadians, who take him home to his family.

Hanna has not come home.

I wait for a week, which turns into two weeks, and then into a month, and when news reaches us about the horrible atrocities that have happened in the concentration camps, I lose hope. Hundreds of mass graves have been discovered by the Allies. Eyewitnesses say it was nearly impossible to distinguish the living from the dead when they entered the camps.

I feel a sense of dread that I might never see Hanna and her family again.

Oh Hanna, where are you? Please come home.

CHAPTER 18

May 1945 – December 1945

It's almost dinnertime when there's a knock on the door.

"I'm just passing through, but came this way to bring a letter from your friend, Hanna Bloch. I'm Bert Giessen," the man says, and hands father an envelope.

"You open the letter, Mieneke." Pa says.

I'm shaking and so excited to open the envelope, that I just tear it open! *Thank God, Hanna is alive!* I read her letter. She will be home in a few weeks. I'm so thankful I finally hear from her. *Please God, send her family home too!*

"Come in and rest, Bert; would you like something to eat?"

"Thank you, I appreciate that, the last time I ate something was early this morning, and it wasn't very much."

"Where did you see Hanna, and is she alright?"

"I met Hanna and Arie Sanders in Amsterdam, at the Salvation Army. They tried to find Arie's family, but then they got the sad news that Arie's family didn't survive. They all died in Auschwitz.

"It's crazy in Amsterdam; it's still very hard to find food and, with all the displaced persons arriving in the city each day, it is slim pickings. Hanna and Arie plan to stay a few weeks longer before coming this way. They hope to find somebody who knows anything about Hanna's family. They haven't found out where they are or if they're still alive. Not knowing what has happened to your loved ones is the worst. When I told them of my plan to head north, Hanna asked me if I could bring you this letter, and here I am," the friendly young man says.

"I was brought to Amsterdam by the Americans, a few weeks after they liberated the prison camp where both my girlfriend and I were taken by the Germans. We were arrested after somebody ratted on us. We helped Jewish children to get to the hiding addresses. I found out, a few days after the Americans arrived, that my girlfriend didn't survive. She died in that camp in Germany of typhus and starvation. I didn't see her again after our arrival, but somebody, who was in the same barrack as she was, knew my name and told me that my Saskia had died. It was horrible—my God, so many people dead!"

"Do you have a place for tonight? You could stay here if you like."

"I thank you, but I rather keep going while it's still daylight. Another four hours or so and I should be home; maybe I can catch a ride with somebody. I'm getting anxious now. I can't wait to see my family, and they must be worried and wondering if I'm still alive!"

"We're very grateful that you took the time and went out of your way to bring us Hanna's letter. We were so worried about her and her family. At least we know she's alive and well!"

"I'm glad to be the bearer of good news. We all need some good news from our loved ones at this time! I'd better be on my way now."

He pushes away from the table and, after he writes down his name and address, he's gone.

"What did Hanna write in her letter, Mieneke?"

I read Hanna's letter to my family.

> "June 15, 1945
>
> Dear Mieneke,
>
> I'm alright. Arie and I are in Amsterdam seeking news about our families. We know Arie's family all died in Auschwitz. It's horrible here in the stations for Displaced Persons—that's what we're called now. Arie's parents' house is as good as destroyed. All the wood was stripped for firewood and there are people living in it, and they don't want to leave, so Arie has given up on it. We're going to Scheveningen to see if any of my Aunt's family has returned, and if they have news about my parents and Davie. We will come back north after, but maybe my parents will return before I do. Since Arie's house is basically gone, I would like to ask your father if he could please secure our house until we come home.
>
> Bert is waiting—he wants to go, and I'll make it short. I love you and will tell you more when I come home. I can't wait to see all of you again,
>
> Love you,
>
> your friend forever,
>
> Hanna."

"Can you do that Pa? Can we keep the Bloch's house safe for them? Nobody could just move in, could they?"

"Nobody here is looking for shelter and I don't think anybody can take it over just like that. Besides, now that we have proof that Hanna is alive, I would say it would be against the law, but I will go to the Town hall tomorrow and speak to somebody who will know for sure what the law is."

I'm going back to school to take a few courses before I can go to college and become a teacher. I'm hoping Hanna will be home soon, so she can catch up and we can start our teaching course together.

Peter is ready to start his studies too. He's going to the school of Agriculture.

"I was bitten by the farm bug when I was working with Peer," he says.

We will bike to the city together again, at least for a few months.

Margie is going to Utrecht to continue her studies and follow in her father's footsteps.

It feels so good to be able to look into the future again, and to make plans that, God willing, will not be interrupted again. *Come, Hanna, hurry up!*

Uncle Jan is strong enough to start his work at the lock again.

Henrika Boonstra leaves Bram and Liselotte with my grandparents and goes to Haarlem to see about her belongings. The house she rented is destroyed, and her furniture is gone. She had a few boxes stored at her neighbors, and is thankful they kept it safe for her. There's nothing left for Henrika in Haarlem, and two weeks later she comes back to our town.

"Stay with us until you find a place to rent. There's no rush, none at all," Oma says.

CHAPTER 19

Dear God, thank you for bringing Hanna home!

When I walk into the kitchen after school, Hanna is there! We hug and cry and look at each other and start crying again!

There are three other people at the table, smiling at us with tears in their eyes.

"I would like to introduce you to my boyfriend, Arie," Hanna says.

"And this is my cousin Greta, and her daughter, Marie."

Arie is a handsome looking man, but Hanna's cousin and her daughter are very skinny and look worn and tired.

"Have you had any news about your parents and Davie, Hanna?"

"Yes, Greta and Marie were in Auschwitz where they met Davie. My parents never made it into the camp. When the train arrived in Auschwitz, they were taken to the gas chambers right away. Davie was taken to the barracks, and the very next morning he was sent to work. He only lasted for a few months. He wasn't strong enough for hard labor, and when he collapsed, the Nazi guard shot him, right there in front of the other prisoners."

"Oh Hanna, I don't know what to say! Your whole is family gone!"

"Yes, they're gone, and so are Arie's family and my aunt, Greta's mother. We don't know yet what happened to the rest of Greta's family—we still have hope, but we waited for so long. It will be a long time before all the missing people will be accounted for. In a way, Arie and I were lucky, if you can call it that, but at least we know what happened. Greta and Marie are lucky too—they survived. Most people in the camps were murdered, and died of starvation and diseases."

"There weren't many people left in our quarters," Greta says. "Most of us were used for medical and scientific experiments. Horrible things were done to the bodies, while the people were still alive and conscious. Once done with the experiments, they were taken to the gas chambers to be killed, if they hadn't already died from all the horrific injuries and the horrible pain."

She continues: "Our liberators came just in time for me. If they had come a day later, I would be dead too. I would not have survived another experiment. Thank God, my daughter survived too and we are together."

Hanna sobs and I can see the pain in her face. Arie puts his arm around her. Nobody talks; what is there to say? But it seems Hanna needs to talk more. She wipes her tears and says, "We have to go on, that's what our parents would have wanted us to do. We were waiting and looking in different D.P. stations, the places where all the displaced people go. Some have tried to go back home, but there's nothing left there for them. Their houses have been given away to non-Jews and most people don't want to go home. They're afraid. We talked to so many and they don't understand, like us, why our lifestyle and positions are threatened. Is it because of our religion, because we're Jews—why?"

"Hanna is right. I always saw myself as Dutch, like every other Dutch person born here, and my religion is Jewish, but that has changed now. We've been uprooted, and many are dislocated and robbed. We have to rebuild our lives and we have to make sure this will never happen to our people again. There has to be a reason why we are still here. Why us? Why did we survive? I feel guilty at times and I have no answer to this question, but I know that my parents, like Hanna's, would want me to go on and try to have a life again." says Arie.

He continues: "We have to discuss what to do next, but this is enough talk for now. Let's be happy and enjoy being together. There is time to talk later."

"Everything is ready for you at your home, Hanna, and there are enough beds for all of you. I'll get a basket ready with some groceries, but you come and eat with us tomorrow," Ma says.

I walk Hanna and her company home and help them settle in.

We all hug before I leave.

"See you tomorrow, Hanna—and all of you, too," I say, and I close the door.

I'm so happy to have Hanna home with me, but so sad about what happened to her parents and Davie. *How could this have happened? What went wrong? Dear Minnie and Sam and Davie, my God, he was so talented and kind. Why, oh why?*

The next morning at breakfast, Pa says: "I have something here that belongs to you now, Hanna."

He and Hank go down to the cellar and bring up the trunk father brought home from the Blochs on the evening they were arrested.

"Here it is, Hanna, the trunk your father asked me to keep in a safe place."

Pa takes the key from his smoking table and unlocks the trunk.

Hanna starts crying when the first thing she sees is a box with family pictures.

"Not all is lost; I *did* belong somewhere," she says.

It's no wonder the trunk was so heavy: The silver is in there, the candlesticks, the coffee urn and, all separately wrapped, the gold-rimmed dinnerware set. All the crystal glasses, Davie's gold watch, Sam's pocket watch and Minnie's jewelry are in separate boxes on the bottom of the trunk. Wrapped in a white tablecloth is the Menorah and that makes Hanna cry again. The last thing we find, stuck in a large envelope, are several letters, and Sam and Minnie's marriage certificate booklet with the names and dates of birth of Davie and Hanna entered in the back by a town's official.

"I need that—thank you, Ma, for putting it in here. I had no proof of identification, other than the I.D. card that was given to me with the Jew's Star."

"I have something for you too, Hanna." I unclasp the chain with the ladybug ring, and hand it to Hanna.

"I found it at your house. It was damaged a bit, but Peter had it fixed. It gave me a lot of strength through the years we were apart, and I'm so happy I can give it back to you now."

"Oh, Mieneke, I can't believe you found it and kept it for me all these years!"

We laugh and cry at the same time.

"And I have something for you!" Hanna says. She gets a bag from the porch, the same bag I packed for her on the night she had to leave.

"Here it is, I made it for you!" Hanna says, and gives me the blanket in many colors. We all have a good laugh.

"It's beautiful, Hanna, and I will treasure it for the rest of my life!"

The next morning we go through all the boxes with clothes, and Aunt Jenny, Oma, Anneke, Vrouw Dekker all donate too. At the end of the day we have enough clothes and footwear for all four of them.

Peter and I organize a get-together with all our friends, who are so happy to see Hanna. Hanna is disappointed she missed the hay-ride and we decide to have another one. It's like old times, but I know it won't last. I'm very aware that every-thing is different; our lives have changed, and we had to grow up too fast because of the war.

On a Sunday afternoon, when we rest in a sunny spot in the sand dunes after a long walk, Hanna says, "We're leaving, Mieneke. Arie and I decided to go to New York. Arie has an address from a group of people who are helping Jews from Europe to get back on their feet. From there we'll go to Palestine and help build the new Jewish state. We have to build our own Jewish country and raise our children there, and every child born will be a testament that the Nazis have not defeated us and can't wipe us out as was planned. Europe is a dangerous place for Jews, and we can't afford for history to repeat itself. We have to build a strong society where we can live together in peace, and from where we can bear witness to the horrible crimes committed against all Jews. It's scary here for us after what has happened and we strongly believe we'll never be safe without our own Jewish homeland. We have talked about it a lot, and many people are waiting in the D.P. stations for immigra-tion to Palestine. Thousands are going, Mieneke. I hate to leave you, now that we're finally together again. I love you, your parents and Hank; you're all like family to me, but I can't stay."

"Hanna, I love you too, and I do understand. We will be friends forever; distance can't take that away from us—and who knows? Maybe Peter and I can visit you over there one day."

It takes a lot longer than anticipated before Arie and Hanna hear from the people in New York. I don't mind; I would like them to stay here for a long, long time, but I'm selfish, of course.

Hanna and Arie need money for passage to New York, for themselves and Greta and her daughter too.

My father and Hanna go to the bank, and Pa takes out a mortgage on Hanna's house.

Finally all the documents are signed, and a date is set for their departure.

I dread the day Hanna has to leave and spend as much time as I can with her. We go for another hayride, have family dinners, and have parties with all our friends.

Hank and Arie build a wooden crate for the trunk and some other things Hanna wants to take.

Everybody wants to see them off, and when we take count we realize there are over twenty people. Unfortunately we don't have enough cars available for that many people, and it's decided that only my family and Peter and I will take the trip to the port of Hoek van Holland.

We organize one more get-together two days before they leave. It's supposed to be a celebration, but I'm very sad, although I try not to show it.

People come and go all evening. There are so many people from our town who come to say good-bye to Hanna. Pa puts his hat on a little table by the kitchen door for donations and it's filling up. Everybody puts something in the hat, whatever they can afford, and it warms my heart to see Hanna so well loved.

When Cornelis Winters, Peer's uncle, who owns the garage in town, comes by, he has a big surprise. "Somebody told me you don't have enough vehicles for all of you to take these youngsters to the boat," he says.

"So I was thinking—here you go, Peer! You know how to drive a bus, so here are the keys."

A big hurray erupts!

"Sit down, Cornelis, and let me treat you to a shot of Jenever! You saved the day!" Pa says.

CHAPTER 20

"I'll send word as soon as we make it to New York," Hanna says when we all stand on the pier near the ship that will take Hanna away. I'm close to tears, but I try to stay strong for Hanna.

"Friends forever, and we will never lose contact," she says and wraps her arms around me."

"Please be happy, Hanna, and if you don't like it there let me know. I'll get you back here, whatever it takes," I tell her.

Hanna smiles through her tears. "I know," she says.

It's time for them to go through the check-in gate.

"Let us know where you are, Hanna, and let us know if you need anything—if so, we'll send it," Ma says.

"I love you, Mieneke."

"I love you too, Hanna."

Hanna takes my hand, opens it, puts the ladybug ring in my palm, and closes my fingers over it.

"I want you to have my ring, Mieneke. Part of my heart will always be yours, but knowing there is a physical part of me that stays with you gives me peace."

One more hug and Hanna turns to join Arie and the others to board the ship. It's another hour before we see them on the ship's gangplank. I lose sight of them, but then I see Hanna on the deck, waving her red handkerchief. It's another hour before the ship pulls away from the pier. People are crying and yelling their good-byes. Through my tears, I see Hanna's handkerchief, and I keep waving and waving. The distance between Hanna and I grows rapidly until the ship is just a little dot before it disappears over the horizon.

The others slowly walk back to the bus, but I stand there for a while, looking at the spot where the ship with Hanna evaporated. A tightness gets hold of my chest, squeezing my heart into a little ball, and I start feeling dizzy, but then I feel Peter's strong arm around me. I grab his hand and start to sob. "Oh, Peter," I say.

He folds me in his arms and we hold each other for a while, until he turns me around.

"Let's go home, Mieneke," he says.

CHAPTER 21

I miss Hanna terribly, but Peter is a great support. After a while the pain eases. Life has to go on.

Uncle Jan and Aunt Jenny come for supper a few weeks after Hanna's departure, and tell us the wonderful news that Aunt Jenny is pregnant.

"We waited for so long, but finally our prayers have been answered! It really is a miracle!" Aunt Jenny says.

"It certainly wasn't for lack of trying!" Uncle Jan says, "Right, honey?"

Aunty Jenny blushes and elbows Uncle Jan, "Stop it, Jan, you're embarrassing me!"

"Well, since this is the evening of good news, we have something to tell you, too!" Hank says. "Go ahead, Anneke sweetheart, you do the honors."

"Hank has asked me to marry him, and we set a date—it's just a small wedding, a simple ceremony at the town hall and a reception at our house after; it's next week, Friday."

"We talked it over with Pa and we'll be renting the Bloch's house. We have to do some renovations and would like to redo the kitchen, but we'll do that after we move in," Hank says.

"Well, you're not wasting any time! We'd better get busy soon with the preparations! Pa, get the glasses out, please, and we'll have a toast to the baby and to the happy couple!"

Peter and I finish our education, and we're both fortunate to get a job in the city. I teach grade one at the Prince Willem School, and Peter is working at the school for Agriculture, a few blocks away.

We still bike to school every morning. One day soon we'll buy a car, but we'll only use it when the weather is bad. We both enjoy our bicycle rides.

Hanna moved to Israel a year after they landed in New York, where she and Arie got married. We write each other often, and Hanna seems very happy working and living in a Kibbutz near Migdal, a town in the northern district of Israel.

She and Arie have a little boy named Samuel, and Hanna is pregnant with their second child. I think about Hanna often and hope that one day Peter and I will be able to visit her.

Soon Peter and I will be married and I'm looking forward to having children of our own. For now we're happy with the way things are. The war has taught me not to plan too far ahead; you never know what life has in store for you.

SIX

Ann is about to close the last notebook when she finds a folded sheet of paper stuck to the last page.

"Compared to most people in the Netherlands and the rest of Europe, we were the fortunate ones."

"We weren't hungry or without a roof over our heads, as compared to the ones in the big cities whose houses were flattened by bombs, and had to suffer unbelievable hardships under the German occupation. However, there are people in our town who lost loved ones in horrible and cruel ways that are incomprehensible in times of peace. We grieve for the ones that lost their lives, and we wish their loved ones strength and courage to go on. We will keep them in our prayers, and we will be supportive for however long it takes. We did the best we could—however little it was—to help the ones who needed us during the war. We feel deep sadness for the ones who couldn't escape the talons of our enemy, but we're grateful for the ones who came home to a free country.

We witnessed the nature of evil. Let us never forget, but instead remember to never be naïve again, and be vigilant at all times. Let's keep the watchmen at our gates to let the Devil and his servants, who gladly share in his bounty, know we're prepared to defend our Queen, our country and our people. I know not all Germans were bad; most of them just wanted to be home with their families, and to those I say, "We forgive you."

"Somebody once wrote: 'I don't hate the people, but I do hate their corrupting governments.'

And I believe he or she was right!"

"Mamma, I love you," Ann sighs, and wipes the tears from her eyes. After she prints off the pages of the book, she puts the copy of the manuscript on the bottom of the box she picked up from the post office. She rolls up the blanket of many colors and puts it, and Hanna's braid, in the box, too.

She opens the silver-colored jewelry box and takes out the small ladybug ring. As she lightly rubs her thumb over the silver band she can feel the tiny scratches. She takes a deep breath, puts the Ladybug ring back in the box, and places it on top of the blanket.

She tapes the box shut and prints the address on the box:
TO HANNA SANDERS BLOCH...

ABOUT THE AUTHOR

Astrid Zoer was born and raised in Diever, a town in the Province of Drenthe, the Netherlands.

At the age of 27, she moved to Canada, where she now resides in Whitehorse, the capital of Yukon Territory.

I was born four years after the end of World War II.

When growing up, I heard many stories about the war, but when young, the war seemed like a long time ago to me.

It was after I moved to Canada, and met many Canadian Veterans here, who fought in the Netherlands for the freedom of the Dutch, that I realized how raw and vivid these war memories remain in the minds of the people who went through these horrible times.

Only a few of these people are still with us, and I believe their stories should be told.

Lest we forget!